To Elizabeth,

Happy Reading!

Betty Grayce

GoForBooks.com

Cats, Dogs and Other People

A Collection of Short Stories
to Warm your Heart
and Touch your Soul

Betty Grayce

Cats, Dogs and Other People

A Collection of Short Stories
to Warm your Heart
and Touch you Soul

Betty Grayce

Published by:Winlock Publishing Co.
26135 Murrieta Road
Sun City, CA 92585
www.winlock.com

Library of Congress Catalog Number 2004104398

ISBN: 1-890461-26-1

Price: $14.95

www.GoForBooks.com

Illustrations drawn by the author

Gentle Reader,

Walk with me, down the gravel path, past the cottonwood trees, through the open gate to my make-believe world.

Listen as my fictional friends speak. If they make you laugh or cry, I will know I touched your heart. And if you enjoy reading their tales, you will touch mine.

Betty Grayce

Dedicated To

DAVID
My husband, my friend and the love of my life

MY CHILDREN
who thought all Moms told stories and drew pictures

TABLE OF CONTENTS

Mr. Wiggins And The Cottonwood Tree

Every morning I walked past Mr. Wiggins' house on my way to school. Until the summer I was twelve, I hardly noticed the cottonwood tree in his front yard or Mr. Wiggins for that matter. I knew he lived alone and that his wife had died many years ago. My Mom sent me to his door, more times than I care to count, to deliver fresh baked cookies. She always talked kindly of the old man but when I thought of him, which until that summer wasn't often, I thought he was just an old grouch with heavy emphasis on the "old".

There were four of us boys, friends and neighbors since kindergarten. We did everything together, starting each day with our walk past Mr. Wiggins' house on our way to school or the park. The summer we all turned twelve, we were full of brimming manhood and ready for action. We didn't know what an adrenalin rush was, but a rush was what we wanted. I don't remember who threw the first clump of dirt at the cottonwood tree as we passed, but soon it became a daily ritual. Some days Mr. Wiggins would spot us and yell and wave a frying pan, "You little brats. Leave my tree alone!"

We'd laugh and run, totally out of breath by the time we reached the school yard.

At recess we'd review our exploits and the dangers we'd escaped. We made up stories about our victim. At first the tales were mild but we needed more excitement so we added to the lies making Mr. Wiggins out to be a murderer with dead bodies hanging in his basement. We were sure he would skin us alive if he ever caught us, so the thrill became bigger each time we threw the clumps of dirt. We tormented him mercilessly. We dared each other to run across his lawn and see how many holes we could dig with our tennis shoes in the soft blades of wet grass. But our favorite act was pelting the cottonwood tree with clumps of dirt. Sometimes the dirt would stick and we'd throw other clumps to disengage the first. We justified our behavior because we began to believe that Mr. Wiggins was an evil man and had dead bodies in his basement. We had become a vicious little gang.

The worst and the last thing I did to Mr. Wiggins' tree was the day I carved my initials in the crisp bark of the trunk. It was on a dare, of course. I had a shiny new pocket knife that my Dad had given me for my birthday. I could feel the hard, cold metal heavy in my pocket as I rubbed my fingers across the design on the case. I had bragged about the knife to my buddies and had shown them the sharp silver blades. Naturally, the dare and desire to use it followed.

I had just finished the last letter when Mr. Wiggins ran out the front door waving a rolling pin.

"You little devils! Get out of my yard!"

We ran! We laughed! But this time I really felt uncomfortable about what I'd done. I guess at twelve, my conscience had kicked in.

Mr. Wiggins had had enough. He went to our parents.

My Dad was furious. I got the long lecture, the one about rights of others and my responsibilities in this world. My Dad is a lawyer so he can really give a good speech. This one was probably one of his best. It included a mention of the prison system and how bad behavior as a boy could lead you down that path. I listened earnestly. I was sure I didn't want to continue down the path I had just taken. Not for me! No sir! I didn't want to go to prison. My Dad's talk scared me, but what really hurt was that my Mom cried, not for me, but for Mr. Wiggins!

She kept saying, "How could you? Poor Mr. Wiggins!" I knew I'd done something really bad.

Of course the lecture was only part of the punishment. It didn't end there in our living room. I had to go up to Mr. Wiggins' front door with a box of cigars I'd purchased out of the money I was saving for a new bike, and present him with the gift and an apology. My Dad stood right behind me so there wouldn't be any foul up.

I thought of the dead bodies in the basement as I rang the door bell and I was glad my Dad was there. I didn't think Mr. Wiggins would kill me with a witness, even though he had every right.

But when the door opened, I didn't see a monster. Mr. Wiggins was just an old man in a plaid shirt and bib overalls. He hadn't shaved and he rubbed the stubble on his chin with a wrinkled hand. He accepted my apology and thanked me for the cigars. He and Dad talked for awhile as we stood on the front porch.

I just kept looking at my shoelaces. I wasn't afraid any more; I was ashamed.

I didn't see Mr. Wiggins much after that incident. I didn't throw any more dirt. My Dad took my knife until I could learn to be more responsible and I walked on the other side of the street, just to make sure I wouldn't be tempted.

My Mom still made me deliver fresh baked cookies now and then. I was polite and Mr. Wiggins was too. But I did a lot of checking out my shoelaces as I stood on his porch and waited as he took the cookie plate from me.

The last time I saw Mr. Wiggins was when I came home from the army with my bride, Katherine. She wanted to see the little town where I grew up and I wanted to show her off to all of my friends. We went for a walk that first afternoon. Without giving it much thought, I headed for the school yard. When we passed Mr. Wiggins' yard, I was shocked at the size of the cottonwood tree. It was at least sixty feet tall. There beneath its sprawling branches was Mr. Wiggins, bent over with a hose in his hand watering something at the base of the tree. He straightened up and waved when he saw us.

"What a beautiful tree!" Katherine always observed beauty wherever she was. "What is the plaque at its base?"

It was then I noticed what Mr. Wiggins was hosing off. It was a bronze plaque with the inscription, "In Loving Memory of Annie Wiggins, Called to Heaven July 27, 1973".

Suddenly, I felt twelve years old again. Shame consumed me and churned in the pit of my stomach. No wonder my Mother had cried when I defiled Mr. Wiggins' tree. He had planted the cottonwood tree in honor of his wife, who died the day I was born! My parents and Mr. Wiggins were tied together forever by that date, inextricably joined by the experience of sorrow and joy. A box of cigars and a sniveling apology didn't seem like much.

Mr. Wiggins and Katherine ignored me as they chatted about the tree. It was just as well because I couldn't speak.

I heard the old man say, "Those top

branches reach clear to Heaven. My Annie can touch them. That's why it grows so well."

I shook Mr. Wiggins' hand as we left. I started to tell him how sorry I was that I had been such a rotten kid, but his grip told me he had forgiven that boy a long time ago.

As Katherine and I headed for the school yard, I looked down at the sunbeams caught dancing in the curls of her golden hair. For me, she was pure joy. I had never loved anyone like this. I took her hand in mine and said a silent prayer, Please God, don't ever make me need to plant a cottonwood tree.

Betty Grayce

Christmas Eve In Rosebud

Fannie Mae Finnegan hated holidays and Christmas most of all. Her back ached and the swollen bunion on her foot hurt like Hell. She looked at the clock on the diner wall and wished the Greyhound bus would get there so she could feed the passengers and close. "Seven o'clock," she said to the empty booths. "Where the devil is Wally and the damn bus?"

The roar of a diesel rounding the corner sent her limping to the window. "Well, it's about time. Little snow storm can't be that bad."

Headlights glared against the crystals of ice forming on the inside of the glass. "Wonder how many he's got tonight? Hope I got enough stew."

She watched the girl climb down the steps and waited to see how many would follow. None did.

Good, she thought as she limped back to the counter. I can feed her and Wally and get back upstairs in time for my radio show at 9:00. Maybe it won't be such a bad Christmas after all. The year had been bad enough, locusts and drought all summer. Not much business after harvest time. She'd be glad to see the end of 1939.

The front door of the diner slammed against the girl's cardboard suitcase, hit her legs and caused her to stumble. She grabbed the back of the booth to keep from falling. Lugging the heavy bag, she slid into the first cushioned seat and heaved a sigh of relief.

Fannie Mae watched from behind the counter. Wiping wet hands on her grease stained apron, she reached for a menu and table service for her customer. Thoughts raced through her head like a sled down Carbon Hill. What on earth is a kid doing out on a night like this. The weather's terrible, radio said, "blizzard". And it's Christmas Eve. She wondered where this kid was going to or coming from.

"Coffee?"

The girl looked up at her.

She can't be much out of her teens, thought Fannie Mae.

"How much is it?"

"Ten cents, free if you order dinner. I got some of today's stew left. It's real good. Got lots of beef in it."

The girl looked over the menu, checking the prices. "I don't see stew on here. How much is it?"

"It's today's special. Seventy five cents, including homemade biscuits and coffee."

"Okay. And cream and sugar for my coffee."

Fannie Mae figured there would be more cream and sugar than coffee in the kid's cup, but she didn't mind. A motherly instinct she'd never admit to churned deep in her soul.

Wally pushed the door open with his back, arms loaded with bags of mail. "Got any coffee, Fannie Mae?" He didn't wait for an answer. "I'll take it to go. I want to make Miles City before they close the road. My old lady needs some help with Santa. Damn kids want everything in the catalog. Must think we're made of money," he grumbled as he dumped the mail bag on the floor. "I'm late and the Post Office is closed, but Hank will pick up the bag in the morning or maybe the day after. You ain't gonna be open on Christmas Day are you?"

"No, don't plan on it. But you can't leave mail here, Wally. Aren't there laws about that?"

"Maybe, but Hank always says, "Leave it at the Diner, if he's closed. So that's what I'm doing." He grabbed the thermos and was out the door before Fannie Mae could stop him. The door slammed in the middle of his "Merry Christmas" wish. The diesel roared with power as the wheels spun on the blacktop leaving a cloud of exhaust hugging the icy street.

"Damn him," Fannie Mae said under her breath as she reached for the coffee pot and grabbed a mug. She kicked the mail bag under the counter and yelped in pain as it bumped her sore foot. Hands full, she headed for the girl in the booth.

Back and forth. Back and forth. The coffee, the cream, and finally the steaming bowl of stew and a plate of hot biscuits. She could feel the swelling inside her shoe and wanted to scream, but she made the trips without a word. Maybe, the girl wouldn't notice if she slipped her shoes off. But she didn't.

Ice formed on the inside of the windows

and the girl moved away from the glass and closer to the middle of the room. She had slipped off her heavy tweed coat revealing arms too skinny and a chest too flat. Was she twelve or twenty? Fannie Mae was curious.

"You need a refill on that coffee?"

"Yes, please."

"You got family, 'round here? Someone gonna pick you up?"

"No, I'm going to get a job and stay here. I got enough for a hotel tonight and then I'm going to get a job and live here."

"Honey, there ain't no hotel here. It closed eight years ago and the only jobs in this town left with the combiners in the fall. Where you from, anyway? What made you pick Rosebud to hang your hat in?"

The wide eyed look of fear replaced an innocent eagerness on the girl's face, but Fannie Mae could sense the determination in her voice, "When I was in the orphanage, we studied about all the towns and counties in the state and I thought Rosebud was the prettiest name I'd ever heard. I thought there would be flowers blooming everywhere and people would be sweet and friendly. I thought it would be warmer too."

"Well, honey, guess you picked the wrong

day for warm!"

The girl didn't laugh. Her eyes filled with tears as she reached for a hankie to blow her nose.

"How old are you, honey?"

"Twenty one." She held her chin up with a bravado that belied the rest of her body language. "After I graduated from high school I worked in the kitchen at the orphanage but they don't need me any more. That's okay, 'cause I was ready to leave anyway. I wanted to go some place pretty, like Rosebud."

Fannie Mae thought of her cat curled in an overstuffed chair upstairs waiting for her and the comfort she had always taken for granted. No wonder the kid looked twelve, the pain of loneliness can do that to you. Everyone should belong to somebody. The hesitation was short, "Look, I got a cot in the store room behind the kitchen. It's warm. You can stay there tonight. I live upstairs with my cat. If you still want a job in morning, I could use some help around here. Ain't easy work, hours too damn long, but the people are nice and I could teach you to cook and clean up. It's not too different from the orphanage kitchen. Just smaller maybe. My customers like lots of hamburgers and beans and they don't mind telling you if the stew ain't good. But a pretty little smile like yours won't hurt none if you work the counter."

Fannie Mae slid into the booth facing the girl. "What do you say? It's Christmas Eve. Better than what Jesus had his first night."

The girl smiled. "Okay. I'm a good worker and a fast learner."

"Hey, I don't even know your name."

"It's Molly. Molly McGee."

"Finish your supper, Molly and I'll show you around the place."

Fannie Mae had only a flicker of doubt. Had she made a mistake, allowing a stranger to move in? She let Wally walk all over her, leaving the mail bag. But fourteen hour days took their toll, just as loneliness did. People came and went, ate and left. They all had their own kin. Fannie Mae didn't have anyone. Maybe, it was the sacredness of the night that affected her judgment.

The store room was dark with boxes piled against one wall. She pulled the chain to turn on the light and shoved some cartons away from the cot to give the girl more room. "Tomorrow we can get this place prettied up a bit. I got an old dresser upstairs we can bring down." She got extra blankets for Molly and said, "Merry Christmas. Welcome to Rosebud," as she headed upstairs to her cat, her radio program and a foot stool.

A chill woke Fannie Mae at six. It wasn't daylight, still cold but at least the wind had died down. She wondered if the girl was warm enough.

Putting on a robe but no slippers she headed down stairs to put on the coffee pot. Moonlight poured through the frost covered windows. On the counter she saw the bag that Wally had left Christmas Eve. "That's funny, I thought I kicked it under the counter."

"What's funny?" Molly was rubbing the sleep from her eyes.

"This bag. I didn't think I left it on the counter. Turn on the lights so we can see."

Molly couldn't find the light cord so Fannie Mae shuffled around the counter to pull the greasy chain.

"It's not a mail bag. It's just an old brown bag. And there's an empty coffee mug beside it. And cookie crumbs all over the counter."

"Look inside, Molly. God only knows what else we'll find."

Molly reached inside the cloth bag and pulled out a big box of chocolates. A folded note fluttered to the counter.

Fannie Mae grabbed the note and read aloud, "Peacefully sharing life with others is the miracle of Christmas. Love and friendship are the greatest gifts of all." It was signed, "Santa Claus."

"Well, what the hell! If someone is playing a trick on us, I don't care, 'cause I love chocolates. Dig in, Molly."

They laughed and thus began their life together.

Many years later, Fannie Mae lay in a hospital bed in Miles City. Molly came to see her every day, sometimes bringing her sons. The boys thought Fannie Mae was their grandmother and neither woman had bothered to tell them differently. Sometimes after work, Molly's husband would stop by, hold her hand and reminiscence about the old days when she had the diner and he courted Molly.

Christmas Eve the family gathered around her bed. The boys were anxious to get home before Santa's arrival and Fannie Mae understood. "Take the boys home, dear. I'll see you in the morning." The wind rattled the window in the hospital room. "Another storm, just like our first Christmas, Molly."

The young mother nodded and gathered

her family. Kissing her friend gently on the forehead, she said, "I'll always remember the miracle of my first Christmas with you."

Fannie Mae watched them leave and thought, "How odd that most people don't celebrate the miracle of family love every day."

She closed her eyes to sleep forever.

The Diary And The Dirt

The attic smelled of eighty year old dust on rafters bowed with too many freezes of winter and too many thaws of spring. I blew my nose and cursed my allergies as I pawed through packing boxes looking for Christmas decorations. The spirit of the season had escaped me. The move was too much and I felt resentment toward Howard for bringing me to this small town in Montana seven miles from the Canadian border. Snow covered wheat fields stretched across a prairie to the Sweetgrass Hills, a small mountain range older than the Rockies, but I had no appreciation for the history of my new community, which I considered a virtual wasteland. This was Howard's old stomping grounds, not mine. His

Aunt Lucy had willed him the house, a two story with an attic larger than our city apartment. I missed the noise and smog of Los Angeles. I missed my friends. Retirement had brought too many changes and now I couldn't find the damn Christmas decorations.

Ready to give up, I spotted a beat up box in the corner under one of the eaves. The water stained cardboard bent in the middle to mold to the shape of the rafter. Curious, I bent over and reached to retrieve it. The top was loosely folded and pulled apart easily. Inside, crystal beads nestled in faded tissue paper. I dug a little deeper and found a bracelet made of tiny ceramic orbs. At the bottom lay a leather bound book with the words, "My Diary," printed in gold on the cover. The little metal lock reminded me of the diary I'd had as a girl. I knew a bobby pin would open it easily, but I felt I couldn't invade the privacy of this unknown author.

Howard's voice startled me as he called from the kitchen. "Martha, we've got company. Come on down."

Company, I thought. We don't know a soul here. How could we have company? The moving van had barely left its tracks in the snow covered driveway. But I didn't understand small town hospitality.

Mary Stewart's coat hung open revealing ample curves behind a flower print apron. She handed me a loaf of freshly baked bread and asked Howard to carry a kettle of hot soup from her kitchen to ours.

I held the warm loaf and listened as this smiling woman chatted about Aunt Lucy, the community and us. She knew Howard, from baby pictures to graduation, military to marriage. She knew the names of our children and when they were born. Aunt Lucy hadn't left out any details and what she didn't know as fact, she made up. I was overwhelmed.

I didn't know it then, but Mary Stewart would be my connection to a new life and oddly enough to an old one. Maybe, it wouldn't be such a bad Christmas after all.

Our grown children came from California, Minnesota and Iowa. They accepted the decision to move to this small town more easily than I did. I overheard my eldest daughter tell her sister, "Don't worry, they won't last the winter here. They'll be back in California before spring."

But she was wrong. By the time the crocus bloomed, I had become close friends with Mary Stewart. Through Mary, I learned about

Montana and Aunt Lucy. I bonded with the state, a rugged panoramic scene of mountains and prairies and a spinster whose spirit reflected the beauty and harshness of the environment where she lived. The house, guarding her secrets, creaked and groaned with its urgency to tell its history and I was ready to listen.

The house had been willed to Howard with one specific stipulation. The flower gardens must be cared for, weeded, watered and new flowers planted each spring. Lilac bushes at the end of the garden must be pruned and blooms cut to encourage new growth. No other requests were made. I was glad of that because the house was a handyman's dream and a housewife's nightmare. At least we could paint and decorate as we wished. Howard was delighted with the prospects.

We heard stories about Aunt Lucy's rudeness to almost everyone in town. As the years passed, she avoided contact with others, relying on Mary for trips to the grocery store. She attended service at the Baptist Church every Sunday, but never spoke to anyone, including the minister. People assumed she was an eccentric, and she was. Stories of Lucy and her escapades made the long winter pass quickly. Each morning Howard and I listened for Mary's knock at the back door, eagerly anticipating the next chapter as we shared a cup of coffee.

Frost finally gave up its grip on the soft black loam in the back yard. Trowel in hand, I headed for weedy flower beds, the sun at my back and a meadow lark's song serenading me. As I knelt, the knees of my jeans soaked up the dampness, but I was so happy to be outdoors after the long winter, I didn't feel the chill. When my trowel struck something hard, I just pushed harder and tried to dig under the object. I thought it was a rock, but as the chunks of dirt fell away, I could see it was something wrapped in a soiled white sheet. Puzzled, I pulled at the cloth and discovered a bone. A baby's leg bone? I jumped back. My throat closed and my scream was just a gasp. "Howard, Howard!" But Howard wasn't home. He'd gone to the paint store.

I ran next door, mud clinging to my hands and jeans. "Mary, come see what I found. Oh my God! Mary, you have to see this."

She let the screen door bang behind her as she followed me to the garden. "Oh, my! Do you think it's a baby? Oh, it couldn't be, could it?"

I couldn't dig any more. Was I disturbing a grave? "Mary, you knew Aunt Lucy better than anyone. What do you make of this? Did she ever have a baby? A lover?"

"Oh, no! At least I don't think so."

Suddenly, I remembered the diary. "I have to know. Come on."

She followed me up the stairs to the attic and I showed her the diary. Pulling a bobby pin from my hair, I easily opened the lock. We looked at each other. "I have to know, Mary. If it is a child, it should have a proper burial."

Mary nodded. I opened the book and read aloud. "The first time I saw those brown eyes, I knew I would love you forever," someone had written.

I turned another page and there was more about someone named Nate and her profession of love for him. The pages were filled with the lament of a sixteen year old professing eternal devotion to Nate. "He always understands," she wrote. "Papa won't let me go to the dance. He says I'm too young. I hate my little sister. She's a liar. I didn't sneak out."

I looked at Mary, "Do you think?"

"Just read on. Maybe there will be more of an explanation. I can't believe Aunt Lucy would have had a child and not say something in all these years. I am the only friend she ever had. Of course, maybe that's a secret you don't want to share."

"Where is everyone?" Howard called from the kitchen.

"Up here, honey."

"I thought you'd be out in the garden. What's the matter with you two? You look like you've seen a ghost."

I was blunt. "Howard, did your Aunt Lucy ever have a child?"

"No, she was a spinster. She was too particular to find a husband." Puzzled, "What's this all about?"

"I found some bones wrapped in a white sheet when I was digging in the garden. I think it might be a baby. And in her diary, Lucy talks about loving someone named Nate."

Howard's laughter filled the attic. His roar displaced some of the dust and rearranged its particles on the cross beams. He reached for his handkerchief and blew his nose.

"Well, I fail to see what is so funny." I was miffed.

"Nate was her dog. He's buried in the back yard. That's why we have to keep the flower beds looking nice. It's a cemetery for Nate. And several other dogs Lucy and my Mom had as children, I might add. The girls were so distraught when each pet died that Grandma let them have funerals and bury their dogs in the back yard. Nate was the last one I remember them talking about. My Mom got interested in boys and the teen social life but Lucy was a loner, ever then. The dogs filled a special need for Lucy. In the animals, she found the friendship she couldn't manage with humans. The dogs, especially Nate, were the loves of her life."

Child Of The Prairie

Charlie White Cloud was small for seven. He sat on a wooden bench in the hallway at the Mission School. Swinging his feet as he bit his fingernails, he tried not to think about what was happening in the next room. Grandfather had been adamant that he should go to school with other kids, so he brought him here to register with the nuns.

Charlie could hear the whistle in his chest as he breathed, so he began to count, first the beveled edges of the design in the dark oak paneling and then the number of boards it took to make the width of the hall floor. He squirmed on the hard bench as he tried to distract himself. The smell of furniture oil permeated the narrow entry.

Charlie looked for a window but he knew there wasn't any. He'd been here before, last year when his grandfather enrolled him. He had lasted all the way through September until the nuns sent word to come and get him in the infirmary.

He could feel the tightness grip his chest as he got up and walked to the paneled wall. He touched the oily wood in a childish attempt to push it back and give him more room to breathe. But the effort was futile.

So he sat on the floor and leaned his head against the side of the bench, wondering why he felt such fear when he was at the mission. It must be the Devil, he thought. The nuns knew all about the Devil. Charlie wondered if the Devil lived somewhere nearby. Maybe Hell was just over the hills in back of the Mission. He'd been told never to go there because of rattlesnakes, but maybe it was Hell and not snakes at all. Charlie shivered at the thought.

His Grandparents were Christian, but they didn't talk about the Devil, so Charlie thought maybe they didn't know much about him.

The wheezing was getting worse. Charlie tried to think of his horse, to remember the feel of the coarse hair in her mane as he buried his face in the pinto's neck. He closed his eyes and tried to picture the river where he and his Grandfather let the horses drink. That's where God lives, he thought to himself. He looks down on me from blue skies and white cotton clouds. I can hear Him sigh as the warm summer wind blows through the cottonwood trees. He speaks in the voice of the meadow lark and watches through the eyes of the barn owl. He comforts me with my Grandmother's arms and wraps me safely in quilts she sews on her old Singer. He teaches me when Grandpa speaks. I can feel His touch when my fingers loosen the dirt around the watermelon plants in Grandma's garden. When I'm home, there's no Devil to fear. I wish I could go home now.

When the door opened, Charlie tried to get up, but he was too short of breath. He couldn't stand.

His Grandfather gathered the boy in his arms and headed for the truck parked in the driveway out front.

"I guess it won't be this year either, Sister." The old Indian didn't turn to look at the nun as he spoke. He grabbed the handle, yanking the door open while balancing Charlie on his shoulder. Gently, he sat the boy on the ragged seat and reached in the cubby hole to retrieve the child's inhaler. The song of a meadow lark drifted through the open window.

"Hear that, Grandpa," Charlie wheezed. "The meadowlark is saying goodbye. He's headed south for the winter."

"Yup, we're headed south too, to the ranch." He patted the boy's knee.

Charlie watched the bird soar high above the trees until it was just a dot in the sky. He didn't feel the bumpy dirt road heading to the ranch. He fell asleep resting his head on his Grandfather's shoulder.

That was the last time Charlie went to school. The State Department of Education sent books and papers in brown manila envelopes to the ranch. Short winter days and long dark evenings were spent at the kitchen table learning long division and the history of this land. Charlie was a capable student but his favorite subject was art. His reward for lessons learned well was drawing paper and crayons. When he ran out of paper, he drew on the sacks that his Grandmother saved from the market and the torn envelopes left from her mail. He drew the plants and animals that he saw on the ranch and captured the lined faces of his Grandparents into crayon replicas. His drawings showed them laughing or quietly reading. He sneaked up on them while they slept and created the images in vivid color on brown paper bags. His fingers caressed the crayons as they rested in his pockets as he waited for each opportunity to draw.

As Charlie grew each asthmatic episode took its toll on his young body. The summer he was twelve, Charlie had his last asthma attack. Coming in from her gardening chores, his Grandmother found him lying on the linoleum floor in the kitchen, his wheezing the only sound in the room. Terrified, she screamed for her husband. The inhaler didn't help and his grandparents knew that they had to get him to the hospital sixty miles away.

Charlie's grandfather lifted the boy gently into the cab of the pickup, his wife climbing in after him. She cradled her grandson's head to her chest and softly crooned songs of his childhood as the boy gasped for air. The old man slipped behind the steering wheel and turned the ignition key. The truck sped down the rutted dirt road to the highway.

When the highway patrol stopped him for speeding, the young officer saw the emergency and radioed for help. He took the old couple and the boy into his patrol car and with sirens blaring raced to the hospital in Miles City. But it was too late. Charlie never left his beloved prairie home.

Months later the old couple gathered some of Charlie's drawings and drove the sixty miles to see the doctor who had cared for their grandson. Over the ten years of Charlie's treatment they had developed a friendship with the young man they shyly called Doctor Jim. On each visit, Charlie had given the doctor a piece of his art. Doctor Jim always thanked the boy and praised his talent. At first the grandparents thought the doctor was just being kind, but on subsequent visits they saw Charlie's drawings matted and framed on the walls in the doctor's office and waiting room. So when he asked them to visit and bring some of their grandson's work, they were pleased to do so.

But this visit was different. Doctor Jim met them at the waiting room door and ushered them into his office. Charlie's grandmother felt emotion grab her as she entered the dark paneled room. She reached for the arm of a chair and quickly sat down. The memory of the first time they had been in that room was overpowering. Ten years ago Doctor Jim had explained what happened to children with asthma, the condition and the treatment. That day, he gave them books to read and sample medicines for Charlie. He showed them an inhaler and explained its use. How many years ago? It seemed like such a short time. Charlie had been a toddler running his fingers around the pattern in the wood on Doctor Jim's desk, his breathing loud enough for everyone in the room to hear.

Emotion choked in the old man's throat as he too remembered that first meeting with Doctor Jim. His thoughts were quickly interrupted by the sight of a middle aged woman with her hand outstretched to greet him.

The young doctor motioned to the old couple, "I would like you to meet Eleanor Worthington. She is the Superintendent of Education for the State of Montana. She is very interested in Charlie's drawings and has an offer that I think you will be very pleased to hear."

Charlie's grandfather recognized the name. It had been printed on the return address of every manila envelop that they sent back to the state for grading. Offer? Why would she be interested in his Charlie?

Her voice was as soft as the pastel suit

she wore, "Mr. and Mrs. White Cloud. I am so sorry for your loss. Charlie was a wonderful artist with a promising future in art. You know, of course, I didn't personally check his homework, but his teachers tell me he was also a good student. His drawings depict his love of nature and the beauty of our state. We would like to have prints made so that they can be displayed in every school.

"You mean Charlie's pictures would be in every class room?"

"Well, we thought the fifth and sixth grades to start with. They'll be matted and framed," she paused, "similar to what Doctor Jim has done. We need your permission to do this. The art work belongs to you. This may be only a beginning. Lots of people may want to use Charlie's art, but you have to decide who and where. We are prepared to pay for the processing and give you a fee for each copy that we make. You own the original and may sell copies to other people."

The old couple exchanged smiles and nodded.

Riding home in the pickup that afternoon, Charlie's Grandmother set her old black purse on the floorboard and stretched her legs. She rested her right arm on the open window sill and said, "We always wanted Charlie to go to school with other boys and girls. We wanted him to have friends, be with other youngsters his own age. Now his presence will be at lots of schools with other kids. I think Charlie would like that."

They had never known that the child had feared the devil at school. They only knew that he now dwelt with angels.

The rut filled road to the ranch bounced them about in their seats, but the song of the meadow lark and the sight of Charlie's grave welcomed them home.

Caring Paws

Frost covered the windows of my hotel room. I shivered as I fumbled in my suitcase for another sweater. Finding the blue wool, I quickly pulled it over my head and settled in a chair to read. But it was too cold to concentrate, so I called the front desk.

"Something seems to be wrong with the heating system. It's freezing in my room."

"Yes, mum. We turn the heat off after nine o'clock in the morning. The business men have all gone to work and it's too expensive. Please mum, you may make yourself comfortable in the lobby. It's warm."

I stifled a groan, thanked the clerk and managed to hang up the phone before I uttered, "Damn."

Glenrothes, a small town north of Edinburgh, Scotland, just across the Firth of Forth, was going to be my home for at least several months. My husband, Bill worked for an American Company and it was important that I remember we were guests in a foreign country and that we not make enemies of our hosts.

I hadn't wanted to take this trip with Bill, but he wouldn't listen to my long list of excuses. He knew I was suffering from depression after my heart attack and I knew he was afraid to leave me alone. I had begun to enjoy my dark cloak of gloom and didn't want to climb out of the dreary comfort zone I had created.

However, I did not want to cause a problem for my hosts, so I took a heart pill, grabbed a book and grudgingly followed the advice of the clerk with the heavy brogue.

I looked around the lobby searching for a spot away from the front door, a quiet corner where I could read unnoticed. An overstuffed chair of questionable lineage beckoned to me. Plopping myself down, I opened the book and was soon lost in an imaginary world.

A nudge on my knee startled me. I looked down to see a black and white border collie gazing up with eyes of different color, one blue and one brown. His cold wet nose pushed the book out of my hands as he wagged his tail. When I looked up, I saw a grizzled old man dressed in a heavy jacket and turtle neck sweater. His smile created wrinkles around his icy blue eyes which contrasted with ruddy, weather burned cheeks. The dog's leash hung limply in his hand. The old Scott didn't speak.

Holding the dog's chin in my hand, I stroked his head and looking into soft multicolored eyes, I said, "Your dog is beautiful. Is he always this friendly?" But when I looked up, the man was gone. The dog's leash lay loose on the floor.

The hotel manager interrupted, "Would you like some tea, mum? If you like, you can have it here or in the bar. There's a fireplace there and it's a bit warmer."

"Where did that old man go?" I asked.

"What old man? There's no one here. The tea?"

"Yes, I'd love some tea. I'll take it by the fire."

The dog followed me, the leash dragging on the wood floor.

Except for the barkeep and four old men sitting at a table in the far corner, the bar was empty. One patron noticed the dog and said, "Well, Sandy. Come to call, have you? Come on over for a pet, my laddie."

I found a cozy chair by the fire and the barkeep brought the tea. My book lay unread in my lap as I watched the men and the dog, wondering where the old man had gone.

When the barkeep returned to refill my cup, I asked him about the dog and his owner. "Oh, that's Sandy, old McTavish's dog. Angus died a week ago and Sandy just keeps looking for 'em. Comes to the bar every day. Dog's not good for much. Angus spoiled him. The only herding Sandy ever did was herding Angus to the bar." Chuckling at his own joke and wiping his hands on a streaked apron front, he walked away, leaving me to ponder my questions.

The dog left the men at the far end of the room and returned to my side. Was it the warm fire or did he like me? I petted his head, stroked his back and wondered.

Every day I went to the bar for tea and every day, Sandy met me. I saw the old man a few times. But he always hurried away and I never did get to talk to him.

After that first week, the weather cleared. As usual, Sandy and I were lounging in the bar, my unread book in my lap, when the barkeep suggested I take the dog for a walk. "Beautiful day, mum. You should get out and breathe the fresh air. I'll have your tea waiting, if you like."

Sandy stood up looking at me eagerly. Why not, I thought.

Our first journey together turned out to be a short walk. I was out of breath after the first hill, but Sandy was patient and every day we walked a little farther. Weeks passed before we made it to the open countryside. I took the leash off to give Sandy more freedom. It didn't take the dog long to show me that staying in that melancholy world I had created for myself was going to be impossible. My own loud laughter jolted me out of my gloom as I watched him chase rabbits, but always slow down a bit to let them get away. It was obvious he was only in the chase for sport and my entertainment.

We followed dirt paths that led us through the valley. While Sandy darted ahead, I soaked in the beauty of lush green rolling hills and flowers struggling to survive by pushing their buds between the mortars in the stone walls. White wooly sheep sometimes blocked our path, but it didn't matter. The sun was warm on my back and there was always a pot of hot tea waiting for me at the hotel.

I saw the old man several times on our walks or thought I did. He was always just a little too far away to call out to.

The end of my stay was nearing. Sandy and I had thoroughly bonded. I knew I couldn't leave him. Who would he walk with when I was gone? Who would sneak him tasty snacks from the kitchen?

I asked the barkeep to tell me about Angus. I thought if I knew more about the old man, I could find a way to take Sandy home with me. Maybe, I could buy him.

"You should take him home, mum? He'd make a good American dog. He's just a pet. Old Angus spoiled him. He's not trained to herd sheep. You should take him back to America."

I felt uneasy about taking an animal when I had no proof of ownership, but I knew I had to find a way.

"What about Angus's relatives. Won't they want the dog?"

"He's got no relatives. Nobody but neighbors came to his funeral. He lived on the dole. He had nobody. The dog's a stray. You should take 'em."

One of the old Scotts who daily occupied the table for four in the far corner came over to where I was sitting and said, "Beg your pardon ma'am, don't mean to intrude, but I couldn't help but hear your conversation. Maybe this little tin box that Angus gave me 'fore he died will help you decide."

The lid was stiff, but I forced it open. The note folded in fourths and smudged with ink read:

Dear Friend,

My Guardian Angel is a dog. His caring paws have led me down a path of love. His body keeps me warm when I am cold. His heart soothes my broken one. He has saved my life more times than I can count. I don't ask the finder of this note to find a good home for him. Instead, I ask you to find a person who needs him. Sandy is a gift from God.

Angus McTavish

When I looked up from reading the note, I saw the old man standing in the doorway. He smiled and waved. I knew it was goodbye and why I was the only one who saw him. I would have known Angus McTavish anywhere. He had blessed me with his guardian angel, because he knew I needed one.

I never saw him again, but I felt his presence when Sandy and I went for long walks in America.

The Gift

It started to rain, that light California drizzle that made the day gray like the inside of an old sweatshirt. Maggie could have turned on the kitchen light, but as usual she was unaware of her surroundings. The house was chilly. Though she shivered, she didn't think to turn up the thermostat. Instead, she put the kettle on for tea, and bread in the toaster.

She was hungry, but she rarely cooked any more. Although her cupboard was full and the freezer jammed, she lived on tea and toast most days. Her son, Walter, had arranged for a grocery delivery service and each week food was delivered. Although Maggie was always polite to the young delivery man, she resented the intrusion in her life. Stubbornly, she thought, I'll cook and eat what I damn well please.

When she opened the refrigerator door to get milk for her tea, she groaned. No milk.

"Damn, now I'll have to go to Woody's Market. And I suppose I'd better go now. It's Christmas Eve and he'll probably close early. Besides, I don't want to miss Walter's call." She spoke to the empty room as she often did these days. Grabbing her coat and umbrella from the closet, she threw her purse strap over her shoulder and headed out to the market down the street.

The rain was steady, a gentle downpour. She could feel the dampness through the soles of her shoes and the pain in her fingers. She looked up and down the block noticing how much the neighborhood had changed over the years. Odd, how she hadn't seen it before. The windows used to be decorated with red and green lights and boughs of holly. The sounds of laughter from families blessed with children mingled with Christmas songs played on victrolas. Now they were rooming houses, with only an occasional light in the window. "I guess people are still at work. It's only six o'clock." Again, she spoke aloud.

Then she saw the dog, a soaking wet ball

of fur with black beady eyes looking up at her from under the hedge at the corner.

"You better go home, doggie. You'll catch your death out here in this rain." She hurried on trying to ignore the dog's woeful look.

Woody greeted her with a broad, toothy grin, "Merry Christmas, Mrs. McClure. How can I help you today?"

"I need some milk for my tea."

Woody had been Walter's buddy all through school. They played baseball and football, not very well but enthusiastically. But they drifted apart when Walter went away to the university. Maggie still felt close to the young man who had shared her son's childhood.

Woody put the milk in a sack and called to his young son, "Tommy, go get that little Christmas tree in the back. No sense in it going in the trash. Carry it home for Mrs. McClure."

"Oh, no, Woody. I don't need a tree. I haven't decorated for Christmas in years."

"You don't have to decorate it, Mrs. McClure. Just put it in your house. It'll make everything smell like Christmas. Hurry, Tommy, we're ready to close."

Tommy grabbed the tree and held the

door open with his back. He smiled up at Maggie with a toothy grin, a smaller version of his father.

"Don't worry, Mrs. McClure, I'll send Tommy back in a week to haul it away for you. Just enjoy! Merry Christmas!"

Sheets of rain poured down as they left the small market. When they passed the corner Maggie saw the dog still huddled and shivering under the hedge. His black eyes pleaded.

"Are you hurt?" Maggie leaned over to get a closer look. "He has no collar. Tommy, do you know who this dog belongs to?"

"No, I saw him around the back of the store this morning. I don't think he belongs to anyone. Sometimes people just dump dogs here. They think the dog will find a home but usually the dog catcher comes and takes them away."

Maggie knew there'd be no dog catcher tonight. "Well, I can't leave him out here in this rain. Come on little fella. Can you follow us?"

The dog listened to the conversation, turning his head from side to side as they discussed his dilemma. He wagged his tail in approval and followed the old woman and boy.

Tommy helped Maggie get the tree in the

house, the dog running in ahead of him. Maggie thanked the boy and tried to give him a dollar.

"Oh no, Mrs. McClure. My Dad 'ud whup me if I took any money from you. But thanks anyway. Merry Christmas." He closed the door gently behind him.

The dog sat in the middle of the living room, dripping muddy water on the flower patterned carpet.

"Well, we better get you dry and some heat in this house." Maggie quickly flipped the light switch and turned up the thermostat. She grabbed towels from the linen closet and wrapped the dog in cotton. She could feel his ribs through the soft terry cloth and gave him a good rub down to stop the shivering. The dog liked the attention. Feeling the warmth of the room, he grabbed the towel in his teeth and tried to play tug-a-war.

Maggie laughed, "Oh you silly pooch. You darn near freeze and now that you've found a warm spot, you want to play. I'll bet you're starving. I am."

The dog followed Maggie to the kitchen and watched dutifully as she fried sausage and scrambled eggs for them both, all the while carrying on a conversation with her guest, "I don't have any dog food so you'll just have to survive on people food."

The tea kettle whistled and Maggie poured hot water over tea leaves in her cup leaving room for milk. Then she set a full dinner plate of scrambled eggs and sausage on the floor for the dog. "We need to give you a name. I can't just be calling you, Dog."

The dog slurped up the food and licked the edges of the plate.

"How about Ralph? I always liked the name, Ralph. Do you like it?" The dog wagged his tail. "Ralph, it is then."

Enjoying her hot meal and tea, Maggie continued her conversation with Ralph, "After supper I think I'll mix up some pie filling and bake us a pumpkin pie. And I'll take that turkey out of the freezer. We should celebrate Christmas with a special dinner, don't you think, Ralph?"

Ralph wagged his tail as he finished his dinner, licking the plate and the floor around it.

"Well, aren't you the tidy little fellow? Turkey it is then and pumpkin pie for dessert."

Ralph's eyes were at half mast as he curled up on the kitchen floor listening to the soft hum of Maggie's voice. Soon he was sound asleep.

Maggie was a flurry of activity. As she rolled out the pie dough, she told Ralph all about Walter and how his father had died when Walter was only ten. She told him about her own job at the diner down by the railroad station where she had worked to put Walter through the university. And how glad she was when she was able to retire.

Her soft voice praised her son as she told Ralph how successful Walter was. She whispered as she said, "No one need know that Walter's mother lives in this creaky old place or ever worked in a diner. It's our secret, okay, Ralph?"

The old house was her home. Had been his too for eighteen years. He wanted her to move. He'd find a "nicer" place, he told her, but she couldn't leave. Her memories were here. "Good enough then, good enough now," she said aloud and woke up the dog. He yawned and stretched. He laid his head back down on the linoleum only to be asleep again in less than a minute. But Maggie was reminiscing and unaware that her audience wasn't listening any more. Maggie had memories to spare and she shared them all with Ralph.

"Walter calls me every Christmas Eve and again on my birthday in July. He's very busy, Ralph. He doesn't come to see me, but he calls." There was a long pause. "Twice a year, he calls." She looked down at the sleeping dog. "Oh you poor dear! Sleeping on that cold hard floor! Come Ralph, come. The pies are in the oven and we'll just go sit in the living room. You can sit on the sofa with me and I'll wrap you in an afghan."

The dog dutifully followed Maggie into the living room and it didn't take any coaxing to get him up on the couch. They had just settled themselves, the dog on the cushion with his chin resting on her lap, when the phone rang.

"Hello, Walter. I was expecting your call. How are you, dear?" Maggie could hear the tinkle of glasses and people talking in the background. "Are you having your "holiday party", dear?"

"Yes, Mother. I just called to wish you a happy holiday. Did you get the fruit basket I sent?"

It bothered Maggie that he would never use the word, Christmas. "Oh yes, the fruit basket was in the groceries they delivered last week. Thank you. I'm enjoying my Christmas Eve with a friend."

"Who? What friend?"

"Well, his name is Ralph. I just met him tonight and I think he's going to stay."

"What did you say, Mother? You just met someone tonight and you've invited him to stay — to stay!?! Mother, are you out of your mind?"

Maggie listened to the agitation in Walter's voice and it struck her funny. "Yes, dear. I've invited him to stay and if we get along as well as it appears we do, I think I'll just ask him to stay forever." Maggie giggled so loud, she woke up Ralph.

"Mother, have you been drinking?"

"No, dear. But that does sound like a good idea. Maybe a glass of wine while I decorate the tree. I think there's some in the cupboard." She could contain herself no longer. "Oh Walter, don't be such a stick in the mud. My friend is a dog. A sweet little dog I picked up on the street tonight."

Walter was still angry, "Well, Mother, if you wanted a dog, why didn't you ask. I would have bought you a pedigreed dog. You don't have to be picking up strays in the street. By the way, what on earth were you doing out at night?"

She ignored the last question. "I kind of

like Ralph's pedigree. I think it's pure mutt. Probably dates back to his wolf ancestry. Besides I couldn't get rid of him now. He brought me the most lovely gift."

The dog brought you a gift?" Walter couldn't hide his sarcasm.

"Yes, dear. He brought me the Magic of Christmas, the Joy of Sharing. I'd lost it somewhere over the years and he brought it back to me. Oops, there goes my timer. The pies are done. Talk to you next July. Bye dear, have a lovely Christmas."

Rosie

The key made a metal clicking sound as I turned it in the lock on Helen's front door. My hands were full of sacks of food for Rosie, so I pushed the door open with my shoulder. The cat came running from the bedroom hall at the sound.

"Hi, Rosie! Are you hungry?"

She rubbed my legs as her answer. Although I am not a cat person, we had learned to communicate easily. There was something about Rosie that drew me to her. Perhaps it was the fact that when Helen picked her up at the pound, I was there. Or that we knew nothing about what Rosie had endured before she was found in a dumpster in an alley down on State Street. That night her beautiful fur was dirty and matted with blood. Her meows were weak, but loud enough to attract the notice of a barmaid as she finished her shift at The Sundown Bar. The woman thought it was a baby or she might have hurried on her way, but the wail was so persistent, she reached into the trash and retrieved the furry ball that was Rosie. That was six years ago.

Or maybe, the cat and I have become good friends because during those six years, Helen has gone on Safari in Africa, seen the pyramids in Egypt, and had her picture taken beside the Great Wall of China. She has cruised the Mexican waters, the Mediterranean Sea, flown to the Bahamas twice and eight times to Hawaii. Helen loves to travel. Her Travel Agent's number is on speed dial. She is gone on a tour or a cruise most of the time. I don't know why she wanted a cat; she is never at home.

Although our friendship dates back more decades than we care to count, I still don't understand Helen. She has tremendous need to be somewhere she isn't. I call it the grass-is-greener-over-the-hill syndrome. She berates me for being a stay-at-home-fraidy-cat. The only thing we have in common is

Rosie and the fact that we have lived next door to each other for forty years.

I opened the can of cat food and set the dish down for Rosie. The fishy aroma filled the kitchen so I headed for the living room. I sat in Helen's favorite rocking chair and picked up the yarn I'd left there yesterday. As I started to crochet, I looked out the front window to see the flowering plum tree. Helen always missed its spring bloom. It had never been so beautiful. The branches, heavy with blossoms, were bent so low the tips touched the grass with gentle kisses as a breeze ruffled through the leaves. It should be pruned, I thought, as Rosie jumped in my lap. I rearranged the afghan so she could curl up cozily and continued my stitching.

I'm not sure how long we sat there, Rosie and I, comfortable in each other's space. I had fallen asleep to Rosie's purring and her warm body soft and relaxed in my lap, when the doorbell startled us awake.

Two policeman! They had been at my house and when there was no one at home, their instructions were to come next door.

"I gotta message for Mary Higgins," the older officer said.

"I'm Mary Higgins."

"Are you a friend or relative of Helen Wilson?"

"I'm a friend."

"I'm really sorry to have to bring you this bad news, madam. There was an accident in Italy. The tour bus your friend was on went over the side of the mountain. Lots of people injured and fourteen killed." He paused to get a breath. Clearing his throat, he said, "Miss Wilson was one of them that didn't make it."

The officer had taken his hat off as he spoke, as though bare headed the words wouldn't be so offensive.

I looked at the lines in his face and seeing how difficult it was for him to give me this news, I felt compassion for all three of us, the messenger, the observer and myself. I felt Rosie rub against my legs. In and out she wove her body through my ankles in an effort to comfort me.

Feeling a wave of nausea, I grabbed the door frame to keep from falling. The officers helped me to a chair. Rosie, as usual, jumped in my lap and nuzzled my neck.

"Is there anyone I can call?" the older officer asked.

"No, there's no one." It was then I knew

why Helen had rescued Rosie from the pound. It wasn't the cat she was rescuing. It was me. She didn't understand me any more than I did her. She needed to see the sunset over the Alps and I wasn't through watching it set over the trees in my back yard.

As Rosie rubbed her head and neck against my arm urging me to pet more, I knew THIS was the world I wanted to see, but I was glad Helen had followed her sunsets wherever that might have been. A tear rolled down my cheek and I wished I had shown her the pictures I took of her Plum tree.

Mr. Tuttle's Furnace Room

The snow blew over the tops of my overshoes and my pants were frozen to the black rubber. Just as I got to the school yard, I realized Shep was following in my footsteps. I would have sat right down and cried but at eleven boys aren't supposed to cry. This had been the worst morning of my life. My Mom and Dad woke me with their yelling. Mom was screaming about going back to Los Angeles and Dad just stomped around the kitchen yelling, "Go, dammit, go. We'd all be better off!"

When they were this angry it was best to stay out of their way, but the house Dad rented was small and it was hard to keep a distance. I took Shep in my room and ate my cereal there. I was supposed to lock him in the kitchen after they left for work, but with all the yelling, I forgot and just grabbed my school books and headed out the door. I guess Shep didn't want to stay alone so he followed me.

Now I really had a problem. If I was late for school my teacher might call my folks and they didn't need anything else to scream about. I didn't want to be yelled at, but most of all, I was afraid they might decide to get rid of Shep. My dog was my only friend and I needed him. At night when we heard the voices of anger in the next room, I hugged him and he washed away my tears with his long pink tongue. Shep was the only good thing in my life. He looked up at me with those brown eyes and I knew I couldn't leave him out in the cold.

"Got a little problem, son?"

Mr. Tuttle, the janitor, had just finished clearing the snow off the sidewalk and he stood there leaning on the shovel. He was breathing hard and I didn't know if he just needed a minute to rest or if he really could help me.

"It's my dog. It's too cold to leave him out and I'll be late if I take him home."

"Why don't you just let him stay with me for awhile. It's nice and warm in the furnace room and I wouldn't mind the company.

What's his name?"

Cautiously, I tried to evaluate the man and the offer. He was old, older than my Dad, a big man with a voice to match his size. The flaps on his winter cap were pulled down over his ears but his jacket was wide open revealing bib overalls and a plaid flannel shirt. I had seen him around the halls but I had never spoken to him before. Since we had just moved to Kalispell, I didn't know if this was proper or not. The nuns at Saint Michael's had lots of rules we hadn't had in Los Angeles. But I was desperate.

"His name's Shep. He's a border collie. He's a really good dog. If he could just stay 'til noon, I could skip lunch and take him home."

"Got a better idea. Why don't you come down to the furnace room and we'll have lunch together. You don't have time to get home and back here. He'll be fine in the furnace room. Come on, I'll show you."

Shep and I followed Mr. Tuttle down the stairs to the basement. The furnace sat majestically in the center of the huge room with ducts reaching out in every direction like branches of a tree. A big table sat to one side with wooden figurines and wood shavings strewn about the floor. Shelves filled with wood carvings lined the walls. Mr. Tuttle pulled an old blanket from a cabinet and laid it on the floor for Shep.

"He'll be fine here. Bring your sack lunch at noon and you can check on him."

I knew it was the only answer so I gave Shep a pat on the back and headed for the stairs. It was hard to concentrate on math that morning, but at least my teacher wouldn't be calling my parents and my dog wouldn't freeze to death.

At lunch time when I opened the door to the furnace room, Shep was curled on the blanket sound asleep and Mr. Tuttle was sitting at the big table whittling away at a piece of wood. "Come on in, son. I'll just clear this table so you can set your lunch out."

"Shep been okay?"

"Oh, yah. He's a good dog."

"What'cha making?"

I could see the shape of a bird coming out of a chunk of wood. Looking around I saw figurines of birds, dogs, bears and horses. "Are you an artist?"

"I'm a wood carver."

When he smiled, I thought Mr. Tuttle looked like Santa Claus without a beard. I didn't feel uncomfortable any more.

"That hard to do?"

"No, you want to try?"

"I don't think I can."

"You can do anything you want to and if you're willing to work at it. See this block of bass wood? There's a little bird locked in there. You just have to picture him and whittle away the extra shavings to let him out. You draw?"

"Yah, I'm a pretty good drawer. But I never whittled anything."

"Well, finish your sandwich and I'll let you use my knife to whittle. There's a bird in there and he wants out of that block of wood."

We laughed. The warmth of the room wrapped around me like a baby's blanket and made me feel safe. Shep nuzzled my knee as I sat at the table and fed him the crusts from my sandwich.

When I finished eating, I took the block of wood and knife from Mr. Tuttle and said, "Where do I start?"

That was the first of many days Shep and I spent down in the basement soaking up the kindness Mr. Tuttle offered. He was easy to talk to. I told him about my parents fighting and how hard it was to make friends in this new school. He was a good listener and it gave me a sense of relief to be able to share my worries with someone other than Shep. Mr. Tuttle would nod his head when I complained about my life. He never gave direct answers to my problems, but he seemed to always know the right questions to ask to make me find my own acceptance or solution. All the time I was talking, I was learning the basics of good design and the whittling was letting birds and bears out of blocks of bass wood. By spring I had a special shelf with my work lined up to show.

My Mother moved back to Los Angeles that spring and my parents divorce was final sometime the next year. When I told Mr. Tuttle about the split, he just said, "Things change, son. Nothing ever stays the same. That's their life, not yours. What's important is what are you going to do with your life?" And he tossed me another block of wood.

When I got to high school I didn't see Mr. Tuttle that often. Things were going a little better for me by then. I visited my Mother in Los Angeles for two weeks in the summer and spent the rest of the time with my Dad.

But Shep was getting older and the day the Vet said it was time to put him down, I really needed to talk to my old friend. I found him in the furnace room whittling away at a big chunk of bass wood and like a fool I burst out crying when I told him about my dog.

As usual, he let me blubber all I needed to and we talked about what a good dog Shep was and how that dog loved to come to school.

That was the last time I saw Mr. Tuttle. But when I graduated from the Art Institute in Los Angeles, I headed back to Kalispell. My friends thought I was nuts, but I didn't want to live in the city and work for some big agency or studio. My grandparents had left me their vacation cabin on Flathead Lake and I figured I could earn enough to live on, so I packed my bags and headed for Montana.

That first morning in my new home, I walked out on the deck, leaned on the redwood railing and watched the waves lapping at the beach below me. The sandy soil, wet and glistening, waiting for my footprints beckoned, but the aroma of fresh brewed coffee filled my nostrils and lured me back inside. I hadn't called my Dad to let him know I was in town. His new wife didn't care for me and the feeling was mutual. I'll call him later, I thought. Nothing is going to spoil my first day home, I promised myself.

As I reached for the morning paper, it fell apart and the obituary page stared me in the face. The words, "Jacob Tuttle", in dark print seemed to leap out. There was a short obituary about my friend and mentor. Services at ten o'clock. He had no family. My God, I thought. No one will come. I looked at my watch and realized I could make the service if I hurried. "No one will be there!" I said aloud.

The church parking lot was filled. I thought it must be cars left over from the previous service, but when I entered the church, I saw the pews were full and people were standing in the aisles. Puzzled, I stood in the back as the Requiem Mass began.

When it was time for the eulogy, Father Mahoney began, "Jacob Tuttle's schooling ended at the eighth grate. He never owned a car, never had a bank account. He lived his whole life in the two room house on the back lot of the church property, but he was a successful man. He touched the life of each and every one of you. That is why you are here. To pay your respects to a man who was important to you. Would anyone like to speak?"

One by one they stood up and related some incident when Mr. Tuttle had "saved their lives". Kid problems, important at the time, trivial today, but they painted a picture of a man who cared about others, especially children.

I listened to their stories and knew I had been blessed to have known Jacob Tuttle.

Father ended his eulogy with the admonition to go out and touch the lives of others the way Mr. Tuttle had touched ours. "That is his legacy to you."

That afternoon, I was sitting on the deck with my mug of coffee and block of bass wood in my hand, when the kid next door came over with a plate of freshly baked cookies, a welcome gift from his Mom.

"What 'cha making? You an artist?"

"Yeah, I'm a wood carver and a sculptor."

"That hard to do?"

"No, you want to try?"

"I don't think I can."

"You can do anything if you want to and you're willing to work at it. See this block of bass wood? There's a little bird locked in there. You just have to picture him inside and whittle away the extra shavings to let him out. You draw?"

"Yeah, I'm a pretty good drawer. But I never whittled anything."

"You can use my knife. Let's see if you can get that little bird out of that block of wood."

Watching the boy carve the chips slowly

from the block, I felt the warm glow of the furnace room surround me and I said a silent prayer of thanks to Mr. Tuttle.

Justice

The sound of the telephone ringing startled me awake from an afternoon nap. The cat had taken over my lap, his nose nestled in the soft folds of my apron and my newspaper had fallen to the floor. I moved the cat gently and rose to answer the phone. I wasn't surprised to hear Byrdie's voice, but her tone made me uneasy.

"What's wrong, Byrdie?"

"Oh, nothing. Come over and have some tea with me. I've got the kettle on."

Byrdie and I had been friends and neighbors for forty years. It didn't take a psychic to hear the pain in her voice. I knew something was wrong. She had gone to her granddaughter's bridal shower that afternoon and I wondered what had happened. Since Byrdie's son and daughter-in-law were killed by a drunk driver, Linda was her only family.

I crossed the driveway that separated our two houses. Pulling my sweater around my shoulders, I rapped on the front door. Byrdie always greeted me with a hug and today was no different. Her cat rubbed against my legs almost tripping me as we moved to her sunny kitchen. I was never sure if her cat liked me or recognized that I belonged to the cat next door.

"Well, how did the shower go? Did she like the tablecloth you crocheted for her? I'll bet she was overwhelmed. Byrdie, it was so beautiful, a real family heirloom."

"Actually, she never even looked at it. She barely opened the box and when she saw that it was something homemade, she just put the lid back on and asked to see the next gift." I could see the pain in her face and hear it in her voice. "There were lots of gifts, Maggie. More expensive presents than I've ever seen at a bridal shower. And you know Linda, she likes the best of everything."

Her shoulders drooped as she poured hot tea in our cups. "I'm very tired, Maggie. Maybe, driving across town and the shower were just too much for me. Young people, they have so much. It's no wonder they don't want an old homemade gift."

I was so angry at Byrdie's granddaughter, I could have wrung her neck. But more important, how could I comfort my friend?

"Byrdie, your gift wasn't just an old homemade thing. It was a work of art, an original design. You don't even use a pattern. Just because you create with a crochet hook instead of a paintbrush, doesn't take away the fact that you are an artist. How many months did it take you to design the mother and child in an oval frame and figure out the stitches to form that image in a tablecloth I seem to recall it was on your lap for months, your fingers dancing with a hook and fine thread. Oh, Byrdie, I'm so sorry. But maybe you're right. Some young people have no appreciation for a gift that comes from the heart."

She reached over and patted my hand. "It's okay, Maggie. Maybe someday she'll open the box."

We drank our tea and talked about our gardens and cats. Linda wasn't mentioned again. When I left, I hugged my friend and feeling her boney shoulders through her dress, wondered if she was ill. She seemed to grow thinner each day.

Her last words to me were, "I'm so tired. I think the shower and the drive across town was a bit too much. Maybe, I'll go to bed early."

She died that night. The doctor said, "She went peacefully in her sleep."

After the funeral, Linda called me almost every day, needing something. I was happy to take Byrdie's cat, especially when Linda threatened to take him to the pound. She sold her grandmother's house immediately, but planned a garage sale before escrow closed to "unload all that junk Grandma had collected over the years". I didn't like Linda, but I felt an obligation to help her. She didn't seem to grieve at all and I didn't know a healthy heart could hurt so much. I would miss Byrdie the rest of my life.

The morning of the sale, I spotted the box, the gift box Byrdie had wrapped so lovingly for her granddaughter's shower. I lifted the lid and saw the table cloth still neatly folded. Linda must have brought it from her house.

"How much do you want for this, Linda?"

"Oh, five dollars is probably fair. People don't use crochet stuff any more. It's really "out of date".

Seeing the shocked look on my face, she said, "You can have it, Maggie, if you want it. For all your help, you should really take your pick of anything here. Just take it before anyone comes."

"No, I couldn't think of taking anything without paying." I wadded up a five dollar bill and placed it in her hand. "I'll be back in a minute. I'll just run home and put this away." I dashed across the driveway with the box tucked under my arm. I said a silent prayer to Byrdie, "Your beautiful work of art is safe with me." I spent the rest of the afternoon helping Linda with customers.

The garage sale went off without a hitch. Everything was gone by five o'clock. Exhausted, I said goodbye and headed for my own house and welcoming cats.

After dinner, feeling tired and especially lonely, I opened the box to enjoy the beauty of Byrdie's work and feel close to her. As the delicate fabric unfolded in my lap, a large brown envelope fell to the floor. In Byrdie's handwriting the words, *To Linda*, were scrawled across the parcel. "Now what do I do?" I said aloud. Oblivious to my dilemma, the cats on either side of me snuggled closer, pushing their bodies to feel my warmth.

"Sorry, kitties, but I have to do this." I stood up, leaving an empty spot on the couch and called Linda. I told her about the envelope.

"Well, Maggie, it's kind of late. Open it and see what's inside. If there's a note, you can read it to me."

The note was simple. I read aloud,

"Dear Linda,

I don't know if these shares have any value, but your grandfather and I bought them years ago and maybe the companies are still in existence or have been bought by some other company. They are yours with my blessings. And I hope they are worth a lot.

Grandma"

"Do you recognize the names of any of the companies?" Her voice was eager.

"No, but I don't read the financial page. I wouldn't know."

"I'll be right over.

It didn't take her long to cross town in her new BMW. I gladly gave her the brown manila envelope and went back to petting the cats.

Several weeks later I saw an announcement in the paper for a contest sponsored by the local museum. There were going to show works of local artists in every medium. A prize of $20,000 was offered. I thought people should see Byrdie's tablecloth. I took it to a local framer, had it stretched and mounted. Every delicate stitch, each twist of thread glistened as maternal love was easily recognized in the images of the woman and child. I wasn't surprised when Byrdie's work of art won the grand prize.

Linda called that same week. She was angry. The stocks were worthless.

MATH

Noah And His Numbers

I kicked a few rocks on my way home from school that day. It isn't every day I sass a teacher, but she was getting too damn nosey. She shouldn't have asked me if my dad was a mathematician. I didn't even know who he was. How would I know if he was good at numbers? He left long before I was born. Why couldn't she just answer my questions on figuring volumes in space and not get so pushy about my personal life? "She's a dumb ole biddy," I said out loud and kicked another rock, number nine.

Two months ago, I would have said, dumb ole bitch, but I'd already learned my grandma didn't like me to use that word. I don't know why, my mom used it all the time.

I'd only been in school two months so that ole teacher didn't know anything about me. And that's just the way I liked it. People don't need to know my business. My numbers are my world and I don't let anyone in. My family was none of her business and that is exactly what I told her. "None of your business," I said. Boy, was she mad.

As I turned the corner and crossed the lawn to my grandparents' house, I wondered how they would feel about me getting in trouble at school. Eight weeks is not much time to get to know people and I suppose I hadn't tried very hard. But I did know I didn't want them mad at me. I wanted things quiet and peaceful so I could count. I lived in my own universe, keeping the people around me in an outer peripheral boundary. The same way I didn't want foods to touch on my dinner plate, I didn't want people touching me, physically or emotionally.

I met my grandparents for the first time sixty one days ago when a nurse wheeled me out of the hospital. They were old, probably in their fifth decade of life. I'd never seen a man as tall as my grandfather. I calculated six feet and maybe an inch or two, with shoulders easily thirty inches across and a neck I would love to measure. He had the biggest fists I'd ever seen, with knuckles bulging on calloused hands. I wondered if he'd hit me like my mother's boyfriend did, but I was too weak to run. My stomach did a flip flop as he lifted me gently into the back seat of a green sedan. I think it was a Chevy, but I'm not good at cars, it could have been a Ford. I counted the grooves in the gray upholstery across the back of the front seat.

Keeping the numbers in my head, I glanced up and watched my grandma's head nodding up and down as she took papers from the nurse and the social worker before she climbed into the front seat. I couldn't hear what they were saying. I didn't care. I counted.

I tried to calculate the square feet in the space where I sat, but the car pulled away from the parking lot so I began counting the trees along the boulevard, knowing I had no control over my life, only the numbers in my head.

Thoughts of my mother kept interrupting my number sequences. The image of her bloody face, the greasy lipstick that I hated smeared across her cheeks and the oozing pool of red seeping through her blouse made me groan for the security of my numbers. He should have killed me too, I thought. I hated the last boyfriend even more than the others. I wish I could have saved her, but she wouldn't come with me to the safety of my number world.

I'd had experience with Social Services before. I didn't care where they put me. I'd found my own safe world years ago. I'm barely in the second decade of my life, but I know the dependability of numbers. As soon as I learned to count, I entered the number world. I call it my number game. There is no emotion involved. At first I just counted things. Then I noticed the shapes of the spaces between the objects and began to count them too. The spaces became as important as the subjects. It was about that time that I became obsessed with figuring the dimensions of the space I occupied in the universe. There is comfort in knowing the area of my room, the depth, the cubic space. I wanted to learn how to figure the air pressure in my space, but when I asked questions, that ole biddy teacher wouldn't answer me. She just had a bunch of nosey questions for me. She wanted to know all about my number game and that's when I told her, "It's none of your business."

I kicked another rock just as I got to the back porch at my grandparents' house. It was number seventeen.

My grandma met me at the back screen door. She had white hair, rosy cheeks and a face like the pictures of Santa Claus, without the beard of course. Her apron had chocolate smeared on the bib and I could smell the cookies spread out to cool. My mouth watered.

"Noah, Grandpa has a surprise for you!"

My stomach did a flip flop and I would have run out the back door but my grandma's hand was on my shoulder and she gave me a little shove towards the living room. I swallowed hard to get the lump out of my throat. Would he beat me with a belt or a stick from the lumber yard where he worked? I wished I hadn't said anything to that teacher. I counted the flower designs in my grandma's apron and tried to concentrate on breathing in and out, in and out. One, two, three, one space, two spaces.

The dog jumped off the couch and ran towards me, slobber running from his mouth, and ears flopping in the air.

I stopped counting.

He seemed to be wagging from the neck down. The tail was just the final swish, like an exclamation point at the end of a sentence.

"Whose dog is he?"

"He's yours, Noah. We figured every boy needs a dog. And this dog needs a boy. We got him down at the pound. He's had a tough life. Needs someone to care for him. Someone to let him know the world's not such a bad place. He's gotta learn there are lots of people who are kind and loving."

I got down on my knees so the dog and I were at eye level. Two swipes with a wet tongue on my cheek and two from chin to forehead, his licks caught me off guard. I couldn't help but laugh as I fell over backward. The dog pounced on top of me tugging at my shirt.

"Well, Noah, looks like that darn dog's taken-a-liken to you. What you gonna call him?"

"What do you mean?" I tried to get upright but the dog wanted to wrestle. I patted his head and pushed him gently, calming him. He sat there cocking his head from side to side, waiting for the next command.

"Well, he's your dog. You have to name him. We can't just call him, Dog."

I'd never had a dog before. I had no idea what to name him. I petted his shaggy fur, counted the four black spots on his back and said, “Four. That’s what I want to name him. Four!”

“Four?” My grandpa sounded surprised.

“He licked me four times, he has four black spots and his tail wags in a cadence of four swishes at a time. His name is Four.”

“Okay, son. Four it is.”

The name soon became Old Four and that piece of shag mop followed me everywhere. He sat by my side while I ate my dinner and gulped the scraps I slipped him from my plate. He rested his chin on my knee while I did my homework. At night I could feel the warmth of his body as he slept with me in my bed.

I’m in my third decade of existence now, but I’ll never forget the day my life made a hundred and eighty degree change in course. Looking back on that time, I don’t think that teacher ever did call my grandparents. Or if she did, they didn’t tell me. The important things I learned that year weren’t taught by the teacher anyway. Two loving, patient grandparents and a shaggy old mutt taught me all the truths I needed to know.

I still count, but mostly just my blessings.

Betty Grayce

What Do You Mean, "They're Gone?"

Moving vans rumbled down the driveway leaving bits of packing material on the concrete. The trash cans, filled with unwanted remnants of family living, leaned against the side of the house, two lonely sentinels guarding an empty space. I thought how quickly a home becomes a building, just wood, stucco and brick when the people you love leave it. I was already missing my neighbors.

My dog, Casey, sat by my side as we watched them go. I knew he would miss them too. No more hugs as we shared our joys and sorrows. No more organ music wafting through the air on summer evenings. And for Casey, no more afternoon visits for a special dog biscuit.

The next morning I realized I was going to have more of a problem than just missing my friends. When I went outside to get the morning paper, Casey followed and quickly ran next door. "Come on Casey. They're not there any more. Come."

He turned and gave me that soulful hang-dog look that every dog owner knows. Usually, he is an obedient dog, but in his own good time.

He's like a teenager who's been told to pick up his room. He'll get around to it eventually. His four paws moved in slow motion as he plodded back to me, head and tail dragging close to the ground.

Age and arthritis have changed his perspective of the world around him. Compliance with my commands occurs when my orders coincide with his desires. Puppy School is a long forgotten memory. We communicate like two old friends who speak and understand in ways the casual observer is oblivious to. Like a puppy, he wants to please and in the final analysis will concede that I am the master, but he expects consideration for his needs. The words, "Come, Sit and Stay" are part of his vocabulary but he expects me not to abuse my position. We are bilingual, Casey and I. We communicate on a level only dog lovers understand.

Thus, I had a troubling dilemma. How do you explain to a dog his friends have moved away and will not be returning? Sign language, body language, neither answered my problem.

The next day, I put on his leash and walked him around my neighbor's empty yard. He sniffed the doorways and looked up at me longingly. I read his thoughts, "Push the doorbell. Maybe, they just don't hear us."

Tuesday of the third week, my patience ran low. I questioned. "Why can't you accept that our friends have moved? I can't be chasing you every morning when I go to get my paper. Just get over here. There is no one there. They are gone."

The dog sat squarely in the middle of the sidewalk. He cocked his head from side to side and looked up at me. My irritation left. At that moment, I understood. A dog's love is eternal. He will wait forever, never knowing when or if a loved one will return. His heart has special compartments for loving all his human friends.

Casey still walks to the corner. He looks

curiously at the neighbor's house. A new family lives there now. He wags his tail in friendly greeting to the strangers. But his nose sniffs the air longing for the loved ones who have moved. There is a special hole in his heart that only they can fill. He waits because dogs don't say, "Goodbye".

The Bully

After my Grandma's funeral, the Ladies Guild served sandwiches and cookies in the parish hall. The room was filled with her friends, old women wearing hats and men fingering their bolo ties or hanging on to their Stetsons.

I didn't expect to see anyone my age and certainly not anyone I knew, although I had lived with my grandparents for one school semester when I was eleven. That was fifteen years ago, but my stomach had that same sinking feeling like I didn't belong. The place reeked of bad memories of a time I'd rather forget. Not my Grandmother, of course, just the circumstances that forced me to live there.

My parents' auto accident caused a lot of

changes that year. My Mom spent four months in a hospital and my Dad was off work for most of that time. Caring for a kid was too much so they sent me to the ranch. I came in late August when ranch work, combining the wheat and barley, is in full operation. I really tried to help, but being a city kid, I bungled everything I tried. I wouldn't say that I was glad when school started but I was relieved. Until I met Barney Culpepper, that is. Barney was the biggest boy in my class, and the loudest and meanest. I was the new kid, so definitely a good target.

He stole my cap the first day of school. Not wanting to make trouble, I told my Grandmother I'd lost it. But the second day he took my lunch box and ate everything in it. From then on, he ate my cookies and drank my milk. He usually ate half my sandwich and threw the other half on the ground grinding it in the dirt with his shoe as he laughed at me.

Barney made my life miserable. He'd poke me on the shoulder until it hurt, and ask, "What'ch got in that box, Skinny? Tell your Grandmother to bake more of those cookies I like." Then he'd laugh. The other kids just watched, snickering, glad it was me and not them getting roughed up.

I can't remember for sure, but I think it was about the second week, when I came home so hungry I could have eaten a whole steer. The aroma of fresh oatmeal cookies baking broke down whatever defenses I had. As Grandma poured a glass of milk, my tears began to flow.

She thought I was crying like a baby because I missed my parents. I did, but that was only part of it. Wiping my nose on my sleeve, I told her about Barney Culpepper and the empty lunch box.

She sat down on the chair next to me and wiped the hair from my forehead. It was a loving gesture, like a hug.

"Well, you can't let Barney Culpepper bully you, Henry."

"But he's bigger 'n me Grandma. He's lots bigger. Nobody doesn't do what ever Barney wants 'em to do. All the kids are scared of him."

My Grandmother stood up, wiping her hands on the front of her apron and said, "Henry, some people think being tall, or big as you put it, is a personal achievement that allows them to do anything they want. Well it's not. It's true you are small for your age, but that doesn't mean you can't stick up for yourself. Size isn't important, brain is! You've got to use your wits, son. So how are we going to teach Barney Culpepper a lesson? We're going to fix him some cookies for his lunch tomorrow."

She grabbed the mixing bowl and held it to her waist as she reached in the cabinet for spices. "This last batch is a special one just for bullies." She poured half a box of red pepper and half a box of black pepper into the bowl and stirred with gusto. "Now in the morning we are going to fix him a special drink in your thermos. Vinegar in your milk ought to take care of that. So tomorrow, don't even try to eat the cookies or drink the milk."

I could hardly wait for the school bus in the morning. Nervous, I wondered if Barney would hit me. As the screen door closed behind me, I heard my Grandma say, "Remember, Henry, keep your wits about you." I knew she meant my brain.

I don't have to tell you how Barney choked and spit when he ate the cookies and gulped down half of the thermos of milk, but he didn't bother me any more. And I stayed clear of him as much as you can in a small town school.

Remembering Barney Culpepper, that

school boy uneasiness came back as I stood there munching cookies in the parish hall and watched my parents talking to Grandma's friends.

Uneasy and hoping we could head back to the city soon, I saw the side door swing open and there stood Barney. I'd have known him anywhere. Almost seven feet tall, he bowed his head as entered. It wasn't a prayerful gesture, he was afraid he'd hit the door jamb. He walked straight towards me. I nearly choked on my cookie as my thoughts went back to that September when I was eleven.

"Henry, how are you? I was so sorry to hear about your Grandmother. She was a great influence on my life."

Oh, my God, I thought. He surely wouldn't hit me here in front of all these people, would he?

Barney had to lean over a bit to face me. I was still shorter than any guy I knew and Barney Culpepper was definitely the tallest.

"Yeah, your Grandmother was a great lady. You may remember, as a kid, I had a hard time making friends. She used to make me work at the church socials. She said I was so big I should use my size to help. Then she'd pat me on the back and tell me what a great job I did. She made me feel good about myself. She's the one who got me started in music. I thought choir was for sissies, but your Grandmother said, "God gave you a lovely voice, what are you going to do with it? Talent shouldn't be wasted." She had a way about her. You knew you had to follow her advice. We had lots of long talks. I wouldn't be teaching music at the high school if it wasn't for her. I owe the direction in my life to your Grandmother."

I was stunned. My grandma had been aiding my enemy.

"Good to see you, Henry. I'll go over and say a word to your parents." Barney patted my shoulder as he left.

It was then I realized, my Grandma loved all kids and she would teach a bully lessons in life as well as a scared little grandson. My Grandma was a special lady.

The Reunion

Physically exhausted from the move and emotionally drained from the recent loss of her husband, Annie plopped herself in the only chair not covered with small boxes. Clothing, with hangers still attached, hung limply over the back of the sofa and shoes heaped in a mismatched pile filled the corner of the room which added to the clutter. She heard a loud rumble as the moving van pulled away. Furniture in the middle of the floor and unmarked containers stacked everywhere were evidence of a shoddy moving company, but they had been cheap. With money tight, she knew this wouldn't be the only sacrifice she and her sons would be making in the coming years. She vowed that the money from the sale of the ranch would stay in a savings account set aside for the boys' education. Without Bert, she would never be able to send them unless she guarded that money. It had always been her husband's dream that his sons go to college. She could not let that dream die with him. She wiped a tear from the corner of her eye, determined not to cry.

The arguing and bickering coming from the boy's room got louder. She knew she'd have to put a stop to it, but didn't have the energy to move. She listened and laid her head back as the voices grew louder. She spotted big brown water marks on the ceiling. "Oh, God, no! The roof leaks! What have I done now? I bought five acres, an old house and a leaky roof. Every decision I've made since Bert's gone is a bad one." The sobs came in a torrent and the boys came running.

They tried to comfort their mother but weren't sure how. At eight and ten they didn't know how to express their own grief.

The door bell rang.

"Who on earth can that be?" She hugged both boys before she opened the door. She was surprised to see two old friends, neighbors from the ranch.

"Sam, Bill! What are you guys doing

here? I didn't know anyone knew about us moving to this place."

"Wives! You know how they keep tabs on everything that goes on. How you boys doin? Like your new place?"

"Well, come on in. We'll make a place for you to sit. I think I can find the coffee pot. Would you like some hot coffee?"

"No, Annie, we can't stay. Looks like you're pretty busy here with the move and all. We just ah," he hesitated, "wanted to ask, well, we wanted to ask you," more hesitation. "Well, we got a problem." Sam was nervously shifting his weight from one foot to another.

"What's the problem, Sam?"

"Well, one of your horses has been stealing mares from both me and Bill. Some of the other ranchers say he's been near their corrals too. We want your permission to shoot him."

"What? Sam, I don't have any horses left. Four died when the barn burned. Don't you remember? That's how Bert died, trying to save the horses. I sold all the rest with the livestock when I sold the ranch."

"Annie, we've seen your brand on his hip. It's your stallion. He looks like that big one Bert used to ride."

"HiBoy? You saw HiBoy?"

"Well, now I ain't sure it's HiBoy, but he sure looks like the one Bert used to ride and he's got your brand. We can't shoot him without your permission."

Maybe, it was just fatigue, or maybe all the worrying she had done this past year, but Annie was suddenly overwhelmed with anger.

"Hell, no, you can't shoot my horse. What's wrong with you guys? If you were close enough to see his brand, you were close enough to get a rope on him. Montana men don't shoot horses. I can't believe you guys!"

The men, uncomfortable with her outburst nervously surveyed their boots. The boys were wide eyed, not knowing what to expect next.

Annie seethed with fury. "Where do you think he's holed up?"

"Well, I think he's up in Box Canyon. That's the direction we seen him heading the last time."

"Fine! I'll ride with you and we'll go get him. Not to shoot him, though. I'll get a rope on him and bring him home." Defiantly, she looked up at the two ranchers. At five feet, she wasn't much taller than her ten year old son.

The ranchers knew they weren't dealing with a child and they knew better than argue. They'd known Annie since she was just a kid riding anything with four legs and if she wanted to go after Bert's horse they knew no one could stop her. The boys watched their mother with new admiration.

It was still dark when Annie slammed the pickup door and left the little acreage she now called home. The boys sat quietly beside her, anticipating an adventure. There had been no arguments between them since last night's visit.

By dawn the horses were saddled and ready for the ride. Single file Bill led on his Roan followed by the boys with Annie and Sam bringing up the rear. They followed the trail along the river and headed west into back country and Box Canyon. It was noon by the time they reached the rocky cliff. Annie dismounted and dropping the reins walked to the edge. Sam followed, binoculars in hand. Annie didn't need any help to see. The moment she looked down at the horses grazing in the valley below, she knew. HiBoy stood a few feet away from the others, head down sampling the grass. She put her fingers between her teeth and whistled, the screeching unladylike whistle Bert had taught her years ago. HiBoy raised his head. She whistled again. HiBoy turned, startled by the sound. The other horses continued to graze. Annie grabbed a rope from her saddle and headed down the rocky path to the canyon floor.

"Where the hell do you think you're going?" Sam was shocked.

"Shut up! I'm going to get my horse. Stay here. You'll just spook him."

The tone in her voice commanded them to obey. Two seasoned ranchers and two small boys stood quietly and watched.

Annie made her way slowly down the path worn by years of animal hoofs. As she neared the grassy plain, she began to speak softly to the horse. She had no doubt he was HiBoy. The once silky mane was matted and dirty. There were ugly burn scars on his back, but he was Bert's horse. The brand, Rafter T, was clearly visible on his hip.

"Come on boy. That's a good boy." She cooed the words as the horse walked slowly towards her. She reached her hand to touch the white blaze on his face. His nostrils widened and quivered as he struggled to inhale the scent of her. "You've suffered, boy. Just like the rest of us, you miss him. The scars on your back match the scars in your heart and my heart too. The big horse nuzzled his nose into her shoulder and tried to lean against her. Tears rolled down her cheeks, she pushed her forehead into his neck. Suddenly, she realized her own pain was less. As she stood in the meadow stroking the neck of the big stallion Bert had loved, she felt his presence. For the first time since his death, she didn't feel alone. A year of sorrow and worry, right or wrong decisions made, didn't matter. Bert was here, beating in the hearts of the woman and the horse he had loved.

"Come on, Boy. Let's go home." Gently, she slipped the rope around his neck and led him out of the canyon.

When they reached Sam's ranch, the men helped the boys load HiBoy into the horse trailer. As they watched the tail lights fade in the distance, Sam turned to Bill and said, "That was the damdest thing I ever did see."

"What? Her going down in that ravine to get the stallion?"

"Naw, that was just like Annie. But on the trail home, you were in the lead, then the boys, then Annie with a rope on HiBoy and me bringing up the rear. When we got down by the river, you remember how the fog moved in? Well, I swear to God, it looked like Bert was riding Hiboy. I could see that ole Stetson he always wore and you know how he rode tall in the saddle. There he was riding with Annie and the boys. I swear to God! Strangest thing I ever did see!"

The Long Summer

The phone's loud ring startled me. I looked down at the mess of wet paper-mache oozing through my fingers and said, "Katie, answer that, please. Tell 'em I'll call back."

The other children didn't even look up from their gooey messes. We had spread the picnic table with old newspapers before we began and now the printers ink was mixed with the paper and paste, but our artwork was taking shape and the artists were thoroughly engrossed in their work.

"It's Aunt Sarah. She says you can't call her back because she's in Paris and you should come to the phone now."

I tried not to let my exasperation show. It wasn't Katie's fault, my older sister was such a bossy nag. Nothing I ever did pleased Sarah. She would be disgusted that I was spending time making paper-mache statues with a bunch of neighborhood kids. Her idea of art was a half hour trip to the Louvre followed by a three hour dinner at some French restaurant, so she could brag to her friends about her knowledge of the old masters.

"Okay, honey." I wiped my hands on paper towel and headed for the kitchen. "I'll be right back, kids." I needn't have bothered with any explanation. They never even looked up from their work.

The aloof and condescending tone in my sister's voice irritated me. "What are you doing? Katie said something about a gang of kids in your back yard. Really, Beth, you need to focus on more adult activities. But I suppose in that wilderness you've moved to, there's not much culture."

I bit my tongue and didn't answer. She wasn't going to bait me that easily.

"Well, dear, we've just come back from dinner at the Jules Verne, a restaurant on the first floor landing of the Eiffel tower. We're going to the Moulin Rouge tonight for a show. Tomorrow we'll be flying to London and on to Edinburgh on Friday. You know, Beth, you and John should be taking trips like this. And you could if John would take a job in industry. With his education, he's just wasting his talent teaching in a small town high school. He's in a dead end job and you ought to know that, Beth. Daddy taught all his life and he and Mom never had anything. And moving to that gawd awful, little town in Montana. I still can't believe you'd agree to such a thing."

She paused to catch her breath and I got my chance. "I'm really busy, Sarah. Hope you have a wonderful trip. Talk to you later. Bye." I hung up and said, "Damn!" How can I let her get to me like that? It's none of her business where my family lives or what we do with our lives.

"Mama! Jimmy's got paper-mache up his nose and he can't breath."

I ran to the patio and grabbed Jimmy by the arm, yelling, "Open your mouth, honey. Breath through your mouth." Paper-mache covered his cheeks and nostrils. He must have been eating it.

"I can't. My bubble gum will fall out."

"Yes, you can. You just did." I wasn't sure just how a seven year old's reasoning worked but I guessed that bubble gum was more important than not being able to breathe. I took him in the house and washed his face, saving the gum on the sink edge so it could be chewed again.

When the washing up was done, we arranged the finished sculptures on the table to dry in the afternoon sun and headed to the kitchen for punch and cookies.

Surrounded by pine trees, our small house was situated beside a creek that flowed in summer and froze in winter. The beauty of the surroundings made up for what the house lacked in size.

My living room always looked like some homeless people had set up camp. Decorated with pillows on the floor and wall to wall kids, it had a lived in look. In winter overshoes blocked the back hall and jackets were draped over chairs. Hand made afghans thrown loosely over the couch were always ready to be wrapped around a chilly reader or a tired dog. Mismatched mittens and caps completed our winter décor to be replaced by shoes and socks of undetermined origin in summer. But the sound of children's laughter and giggles filled the room year round. And the aroma of cookies in the oven or hot dogs on the grill permeated the air inside or out. I wasn't going to let my older sister invade my precious territory.

The next day, I lined all the paint pots down the center of the picnic table. With new newspaper laid carefully it looked clean and orderly. I knew the neatness wouldn't last and by nine o'clock the neighbor kids and mine gathered for more activity. Each chose a favorite spot and gleefully settled in, brush in hand. It always amazed me how quiet they could be when they concentrated on their work. The poking and nudging disappeared and their voices dropped an octave.

"Can we do a puppet show with our statues? Mine is a monster and he could be the villain." Jimmy, the bubble gum kid, was full of ideas.

"Why not?" I looked at the eager faces before me and knew our next project would be a show.

One activity led to another that summer. Imagination was our only guide. Nine little boys and girls cemented friendships over glue, paint, paper-mache and stories told and acted out.

As the weeks continued so did my sister's phone calls. I tried to ignore her criticism, but it was getting to me. I didn't tell John because I knew he would be angry. I was too, but I didn't know how to stop her meddling. With each call I grew more irritated.

The last week of August, John and I decided to have a cook-out to celebrate the end of summer. All the neighbors were invited and we decorated the back yard with crepe paper streamers and lights strung from the tree branches. The kids decided their parents should see their art work so they taped their paintings to the side of the garage and placed their painted sculptures on benches.

Jimmy said, "It's just like a moo-sium." And he was right.

Just as I patted him on the head, I heard the timer go off and ran to get cookies out of the oven. When the phone rang, I had a sinking feeling it was Sarah. "I just wanted to let you know, I'm home in Los Angeles. I've had a marvelous time traveling. And little sister, what can you say for your summer? How did you spend your time?" she said sarcastically.

With the smell of chocolate chips in my nostrils, I suddenly knew how to answer her. "Sarah, remember how Dad always like to put puzzles together? Well, I figure life is a bit like a big puzzle. We fit pieces together each day and eventually finish the whole picture. This summer I've been helping my children put the pieces of their childhood together. We've been busy making memories."

There was a long silence. I almost said goodbye and hung up when I heard her voice, soft and childlike, "Daddy was good to us, wasn't he, Beth? He and Momma always had time for us, didn't they?"

"Yes, Sarah. They always made time for us. We were the focus of their lives. They were good parents."

"You and John are good parents, too. Maybe, I'll come and see you sometime. See that little town you live in." Her laugh was weak and forced.

"I think that would be a good idea, Sarah. We'll remember the good times we had as kids."

"Yah, the pieces Daddy and Momma put together in our puzzle. I'll call you. Bye."

I hung up the phone and went back to my family knowing I wouldn't dread her next phone call.

Voices From The Ashes

Reduced to ashes and surrounded by a silhouette of stately pines, I groaned. The acrid smell of smoke permeated the only wall left standing, its plaster stained black with soot. "Oh," my sound blended with a soft breeze rustling in the cold night air.

"What are you groaning about?" said the stone fireplace, the voice echoing out the chimney.

"Me? I'm nothing but a pile of pulverized wood, cabinets, carpets and furniture. At least you're still standing." Angrily I said, "You're dirty and ugly, but your stones still rise to the sky to welcome the family home, but I've burned to the ground. My life is over. There's no cabin here any more. My hand woven rugs on hardwood floors, windows overlooking the valley, are all gone. I'm nothing but a lot," I moaned.

The chimney was silent for awhile. "You're feeling sorry for yourself because you're not a home any more?"

"Of course! How would you feel if you weren't a fireplace and chimney any more? What if your stones had tumbled all over the living room floor in that last earthquake? You were plenty worried then. I heard your sighs of relief when the shaking stopped. So don't give me that, "What are you feeling so bad about?" I used to be a home. That's what I'm feeling. Empty! That's it, I'm empty."

The chimney reflected the white moon light. The black outline of skeleton trees faded into the mist behind the stony structure. Quietly, the fireplace spoke, "Your home is still here. Just because the fire destroyed the cabin it doesn't mean your home is lost. Home isn't a house. It's the people in it. They'll be back to build you new walls and windows. Our roots go deeper in the earth than the pines that surrounded us. The laughter of the children who grew up here reverberates through the blackened forest as we speak. Cabin, you are more than a pile of ashes on the ground.

You are a home, the core and heart of a family. The house burned, but home is the family. They'll be back.

Air stirred. Debris drifted over my foundation. I heard cars coming up the dirt road. Headlights flashed on a sign in the back of a pick up. Ashes blew over its hastily printed words, but I could make them out. WE'LL BE BACK, it read.

I watched my family pound a stake in the dirt for the sign they'd brought up the mountain. Their strong voices echoed in the wounded trees as they planned the future and soothed my aching heart. I watched them drive away knowing they'd return.

The fireplace said, "I hope they build me a new mantle, an oak one, maybe."

I sighed.

The night was quiet except for the retreating cars, the beating of my heart and the sound of gentle rain beginning to fall.

The Killer

The old woman kicked the beer cans aside and grabbed the back of a chair for support. A broken whiskey bottle lay on the floor. Blood dripped from her hand as she picked up the phone. Her breath came in deep gasps as she dialed the sheriff's office.

The phone call complete, she stepped over the body and groped her way to the front door, the rifle still in her hand. She pushed the screen door open to let the dog go out ahead of her. Using the rifle as a cane, she hobbled to a wicker chair on the porch. As she sat rocking back and forth, her breathing became easier.

The sun was setting. She shivered, but felt the warmth of calmness surround her. The blood dried, but the black and blue marks still vivid, were getting darker. Her body ached from beatings long since past. Her spirit was broken from years of abuse, passively accepted as her lot in life.

Bordered by corn fields, a long dirt road stretched before her. It would be at least an hour before the sheriff would arrive. But it didn't matter to her. She listened as the evening birds flocked to the tops of the cottonwood trees to nest for the night. "God's creatures", she said aloud to the stillness of twilight. The rocking chair squeaked with movement. She wiped her brow and pushed the white strands of hair from her forehead as she reached down to pet the old dog at her feet.

"It's gonna be okay, Shep. Don't you worry none. It'll be okay."

She watched the ribbons of pink clouds turn to mauve as the sun set and the evening star twinkled its greeting. The sky became darker. A thousand stars became diamonds as they captured her imagination. She rocked slowly as she rested and waited.

The sound of gravel ground beneath the tires and bright headlights broke into her reverie. The dog began to bark.

"You called us, Miz Hawkins?" Seeing the rifle lying inert across the old woman's lap, the sheriff stood calmly by his patrol car as he called out to her.

"Yes, um. He's on the floor in the living room. Here's the gun what done it." She stood up slowly, and with the barrel pointed down, handed the rifle to the sheriff.

Her voice was firm as she spoke, "Will you take ole Shep over to Widow Brown's? She'll take good care of him while I'm gone. She's got four dogs. Won't hardly notice one more."

"Sure, we'll take care of Shep."

She remembered the spinning feeling as she fell and the strong arms of the Sheriff as he caught her. The sharp pain across her ribs, just before her world became black was etched in her memory.

The hospital room smelled like laundry soap. She had never seen walls so white. She was uneasy, but the voices outside her room were familiar.

Widow Brown pushed the door open and stood beside her bed. "You look terrible!" Her giggle made Selma laugh.

"Well, I guess I probably do. How's Shep? Did the Sheriff bring him over to you?"

"Yes, he's fine. You'll see for yourself in a

few days. That ole fool dog been chasing rabbits and showing my dogs all kinds of mischief tricks."

"Hattie, I'll be going to jail, I reckon. They aint gonna let me go home."

"Nonsense, everyone knows how he beat you day and night for years. Your face still looks like raw beefsteak. With broken ribs and a concussion the DA says it was self defense. He ain't gonna file any charges. You're going home soon as you get well."

The nurse pushed the door open with her back, her hands full with a tray of meds.

"I best be going now, Selma. But I'll be back tomorrow. They'll be letting you go home soon."

Selma lay quietly on her side as the nurse gave her the shot to take the pain away. She couldn't remember a time when anyone had treated her so kindly. Her bruised hand caressed the pillow as she thought of the words her friend has just said.

Self defense? She knew it wasn't self defense. She had never defended herself in all those years of marriage. Weekly beatings and daily tirades were her life sentence. She had endured it for forty years. This was her first defiant act, but he shouldn't have kicked Shep.

He never should have laid a boot on him. Her bruised hand made a fist against the white linen as she whispered, “It weren’t no self defense; it was SHEP DEFENSE. Nobody hurts my dog.”

Betty Grayce

Turning Corners

When the phone rings at two AM on a Tuesday morning, you know it's not going to be good news. I rolled over and for a few seconds pretended I didn't hear it. I would have put the pillow over my head like a kid, but I knew that wouldn't help, so I grabbed the damn thing off the hook and said, "Yah?"

The voice on the other end was my little brother, Frankie. "Henry, Dad's had a heart attack. I think you better come home."

I sat up in bed fully awake. "When? How'd it happen? How is he? Where is he now?"

I'm a reporter for the LA Times and I can ask better questions than that, but emotion makes you dumb as dirt. "I'll get a flight out as soon as I can. Call you back as soon as I know when."

For five minutes, I sat on the edge of the bed, thoughts racing in my brain but my body completely immobilized. My Dad had never been sick a day in his life. He was the toughest old hombre I'd ever met. He made my drill sergeant sound like a choir boy. Dad was the County Sheriff back home in Forsyth, Montana. It's a small town and we never had much crime which I attributed to the fact that lots of people were scared of my Dad. I sure was.

The flight takes about three hours with a layover in Salt Lake. I had plenty of time to think, too much time. I was afraid to fall asleep because I didn't want the dream to come and then wake up shaking and covered in sweat. I don't know why I relive that moment in my life over and over again in my dream, but when there's stress I can count on the dream girl to be there looking at me with wounded eyes as her soul enters mine.

I remember when it happened more clearly than I can recall my morning coffee. It was the crime of the century in our small town and the day I turned the corner in life that ended my childhood. I was thirteen.

Frankie and I were headed for the river that morning. School was out and we had the whole summer before us. Dad said we had to work our paper route, but other than that and a few chores Mom gave us, fishing and hanging out at the ball field were going to be top priority. Frankie's a year younger than I am, but he was always bigger and stronger. I had polio when I was four and everyone said that was why, but I think Frankie took after Dad, big and husky, and I was always going to be scrawny like Mom. Size never mattered to us. We did everything together. He was the jock and I was the nerd, but we were buddies.

We were about a quarter of a mile into the woods and I could see the Yellowstone River through the cottonwood trees when Frankie said, "What's that stink, Henry?

"I don't know. Something dead, I suppose. A squirrel maybe or a raccoon."

I turned in the direction of the stench and that's when I saw her. She stared right at me or through me. Her naked body was twisted, legs stretched to the side and her arms reached over her head. There was black, dried blood on her face. Her open mouth screamed a silent cry.

I'd never seen a dead body before and my feet felt like they were made of stone. I couldn't move.

Frankie came pushing in behind me, "Henry, she's dead, ain't she? Let's go get someone."

He turned and ran for help, but I was caught, frozen by emotion. I'd never seen a naked girl before. I looked at her bare breasts and my face flushed with embarrassment. That's when I looked into her eyes, wide open looking back at me. I took off my shirt and covered her body. I stayed until my Dad came. He gave me hell for disturbing a crime scene, but I wasn't listening. His voice was just a roar. Other deputies came and Frankie and I were sent home.

Lots of things changed that summer. Frankie was a hero and he basked in the limelight. He had always been the star in our family. He was the best pitcher on the town baseball team. Dad said he was good enough to go pro. He didn't, but Dad thought he could have. Frankie wound up as the high school coach and Dad never missed one of his games.

I was always a different kind of kid. I liked the library better than the ball park and I don't think my Dad ever forgave me for that.

Listening to Frankie tell the guys over and over again the story about the naked, dead girl, I felt sick. Frankie hadn't seen her eyes.

I guess he was too busy looking at her tits. And that's the part the boys wanted to hear about. Some mention was always made about me disturbing the crime scene. It made me feel dumb, but worse than that, I couldn't get the girl out of my mind. I cursed myself for looking into her eyes and binding myself to her for eternity. I wanted to know who she was; I wanted to know her.

Even when they found her killer, it didn't satisfy me. I overheard my Dad tell my Mom that the girl was a half breed, lived down on the island. Her family would take care of the burial when the coroner didn't need the body any more for evidence. Her name was Callahan. Breezy Callahan. My Dad said, "Hell-of-a name for a girl."

That's all I ever knew about her, but I couldn't let her go. I was glad Frankie and I didn't share a room, because he wouldn't understand a brother plagued with nightmares and cold sweats every night. He'd think I was nuts and I did too, but then, he hadn't looked into her eyes.

The drone of the engine was lulling me into a reverie of the past. Flying always made me sleepy and I fought to stay awake. I thought of all the corners I had turned on my path of life. The twists and turns that I chose or were chosen for me.

In high school, my grades were so-so. I couldn't blame Breezy Callahan for that, but a good night's sleep might have helped. Not until I was a senior, and I had Mrs. Evens for English Lit, did anyone ever ask me why I never got anything beyond a C. I'll never forget the afternoon she said to me, "Henry, why do you strive to be mediocre when you could be outstanding?" I hadn't really thought about it, but that's the day, I turned another corner and began to apply myself at school.

Frankie met me in Billings. He filled me in on the details on the ride down to Forsyth. I tried to listen, but fatigue eventually took its toll and when he pulled up in front of the hospital, he had to wake me.

"We're here, Henry. I thought you'd like to see him before I took you home."

"Yah,"

The Intensive Care Unit was quiet except for the bleeping of machines and the soft voices of two nurses. I was intimidated by the sight of my Dad hooked up to IV's and oxygen. Frankie gave me a nudge and I moved closer.

"Dad?"

"Henry? That you?" His voice was barely

audible. He reached for my hand and I took his. He wasn't big and powerful any more. His smile told me he was glad I had come. I don't know how long I stood there holding his hand in mine, but as I watched, he closed his eyes and I knew he was gone.

Again, my feet felt like they were made of stone. I couldn't move. But this time was different. My Dad was at peace. His closed eyes set me free.

Frankie went to get us some coffee while I sat in a small waiting room. The nurse from Intensive Care came in to talk to me.

"I just wanted to let you know how proud of you your Dad was. When he first came in, he kept telling us all about his two sons, the one who lives here and the one who is a reporter for the LA Times. He would smile and say, "Henry, that boy of mine, always did see and feel things others missed. He's a great writer, you know. You'll be reading one of his novels some day." He was very proud of you. I just wanted you to know that."

I looked up at her and thought, I know her from somewhere, but my mind was a blur.

She started to walk away, but paused at the door and came back. "Henry, I'm Breezy Callahan's little sister. I've heard the story about how you and your brother found her and," she paused. She seemed embarrassed. "Well, I just want to thank you for covering her up with your shirt."

As Breezy Callahan looked at me through the soft brown eyes of her sister, she released my soul. I knew I wouldn't be having the dream any more.

That was the moment, all the pieces of my life fell into place. I turned that final corner and knew I'd be okay. My Dad had loved me all along. He knew we were different, but he loved me anyway.

The Meek Clan

Flames licked through the smoke covered earth and dealt death to all who remained. God had lost his patience with humans who were engulfed in greed and worshiped the power of gold. True to his word, this time not a flood, but fire consumed the surface of the planet.

Volcanoes erupted and earthquakes cracked the crust. Small groups of humans, simple in their ways and pure in their hearts ran for giant holes in the hills and dales seeking safety. Deep into the interior they fled, carrying all their belongings, beloved animals at their heels.

The walls of the caves were cold and damp. The smell of musky interiors mixed with the acrid vapors urged them on. Deeper and deeper they went, into the bowels of the planet.

They came from every curve of the earth's globe and met in large open rooms near the core. Frightened at their first encounters with other clans, they made up a common language to communicate. They learned to speak to the animals as well as each other. Even the lion forgot his roar. Peace reigned in this internal world as generations lived together and learned to adapt to their environment.

The magnetic core gave off heat, providing a constant comfortable temperature. They ate grasses and algae and drank water form the deep lakes that dotted many of the caverns. They became vegetarians. The animals were their friends.

They had no way to measure time and no need to. People grew old and died. Babies were born to replace them.

After the first century, a pressing need developed. The boy was aware of the danger. He watched his grandfather sitting by the open fire, and knew that he must speak to him.

The old man brushed the white hair from his brow as he leaned forward to hear his grandson's voice. His beard trailed on a dusty rug where he sat, his arms folded in his lap.

A worn blanket draped across his boney shoulders. Sheep grazed quietly in a small alcove. A lion stretched his back and curled his paw around the old man's foot.

"Grandfather, the time has come. We must make plans to go on a new journey. The air in our cave does not contain enough oxygen. We are sleepy and tired all the time."

The boy looked anxiously at the old man who petted the lion gently as he spoke, "Our ancestors brought us here many years ago for our safety. The Bible tells us how God destroyed the evil. The earth is afire. Flames are consuming everything. It is not safe to leave."

"It is not safe to stay, Grandfather. How many generations have lived in these deep caves? As our clan and animals grew in numbers, we needed to go farther down in new passages. Let me go with your blessing and I will find another place for us to live."

The boy looked around at the group of trusting, peace loving souls. The animals listened, not speaking. Birds lit on perches high on the walls or fluttered near the blackened ceiling. The people, quiet with concern, trusted the boy. Their worried faces gave him strength to continue his quest.

"Grandfather, I will go for a short time. If I find no other place for us, I will return and we will all die together in our cave. It will be God's will. But I feel this urgency to go. Perhaps, it is God's will that I do."

The old man reached a wrinkled hand to touch the boy and said, "Son, you have been our light and guidance since the day you were born. I don't understand how you know these things, but you were born with knowledge far beyond anything we understand. I trust you, as the gift from God you have been since your birth. You have brought beauty to our cave deep in the heart of earth. Until you came, we lived with only the mud and stone surrounding us. Now paintings adorn every wall with blue and green made from cobalt and zinc. We heard no music until you made flutes from hollow reeds. Your algorithms make patterns we don't understand but we know the designs spread up and down our walls tell stories that are meaningful to you. Go with my blessings, son."

The boy stood facing the clan and said, "I will take my dog and return soon. Prepare your treasures, as we will make a caravan and move to a safe haven."

There was no dissent. They did not understand but they trusted the boy. As he quickly prepared for the journey, members came to gently hug and pray for him. As they held his hand for a long moment or embraced him, he noted their weakness and knew there was no time to waste. The dog also sensed the urgency and nudged his master's knee to hurry. Lighting a torch from the communal fire he grabbed his woven bag. Looking back at the ones he loved, he left the group knowing it was his and their only hope.

The first part of the climb was a gentle slope but as the boy continued, the slippery rocks made the ascent more difficult. He reached a ledge and stopped to rest. Gently pulling the dog beside him, he opened the bag his mother had given him and shared his food with his four legged friend. The dog thanked him with a few licks to the cheek and snuggled down for a short nap.

The boy thought about the time element he had given the old man. He knew the clan knew nothing about time. Short or long, neither would have any meaning. He would have to calculate his absence and return before they became worried and frightened. Kindness to each other was a basic law of the cave.

He roused the dog and continued his climb.

Unsure how long he'd rested, he hurried on. Soon a wisp of light far ahead cut through the blackness. Knowing it would be dangerous to put the torch out, he held it high. The rough edges of a boulder jabbed his shoulder, scraping the skin. He felt the warm blood oozing down his arm, but a blinding light streamed through the opening of the cave and distracted him from any pain.

"Oh, my God!" he said aloud. A beautiful valley stretched before him. He had never seen such color. The vibrancy and pattern of light made him squint. His coughing doubled him over as he tried to breathe the fresh air. Fields of grasses waist high beckoned to him.

The dog ran and jumped as green blades tickled his belly and the sun warmed his back.

The journey back was faster and easier. The people, ready for travel, awaited him. The boy was amazed at the trust they had in him. He knew it was God who was in the lead.

It took much longer to reach the top this time. There were many stops and rests, but no complaints. When they reached the lush valley, one by one they knelt and thanked God for their deliverance.

The old grandfather rested on a rock, his legs outstretched and tall grass surrounding him. The boy sat beside him and gently patted his knee. The old man spoke, "How did you know?"

The boy answered, "It was in the Bible, Grandfather. Jesus taught the disciples, The Beatitudes. When he said, "Blessed are the meek, for they will inherit the earth," I knew He meant us. We are the Meek."

Betty Grayce

Ghosts In The Cupboard

The rumble of the morning freight train shook the hot coffee in my cup, spilling some on the oilcloth. Dishes rattled in the cupboards, but I didn't notice. My life was measured by the rhythm of the steam engines that pulled the freights and passenger cars only a few yards from my back lawn.

Forty years ago we'd bought the house because it was big and cheap. With three sons and a baby on the way, I didn't think any outside noises could disturb me. And they didn't. The railroad and I existed in perfect harmony. The seven o'clock freight was better than any alarm clock. The little ones slept and woke to the railroad schedule and grew to be adults. The gentle motions that rocked the house blended with my soul and became part of the pattern of my days.

They came yesterday, all three sons with their spouses and Lily May my grown-up baby girl. They came to celebrate my seventieth birthday. "It's a big day, Mom," Tom Junior said. "We all wanted to be here." A big man, like his father, he commanded an audience. His brothers and sister let him speak for everyone. He was a leader, always had been.

But I knew my eldest and I knew the real reason they were here, all at the same time. I'd seen the brochures Tom had mailed to me. They wanted me to sell the house and move closer to one of them.

"Assisted living," Tom said. "Seattle or Los Angeles," they didn't care. Ever since their Dad died, they wanted me out of my house and somewhere they could care for me, or watch me. Assisted living, indeed! As if I didn't know how to live by myself. I'd been a widow for five years. There wasn't anything I didn't know about living alone.

The train puffed away leaving my kitchen and me nestled in a cozy silence. I got up and poured myself another cup of coffee. I thought of Lily May, my youngest, sleeping in her old bedroom upstairs. She hadn't brought a boyfriend with her this time and I was thankful. Her brothers had never approved of her choices in men and I had to admit, I didn't much like them either.

I heard the thumps as feet came down the wooden stairs. Rubbing the sleep from her eyes and looking like a twelve year old in her pink, chenille bathrobe, Lily May's stood in the kitchen doorway. "Momma, I forgot how loud that damn train could sound. How can you stand the noise?"

"You get used to it, honey. It never bothered you when you lived at home. Want some coffee?"

"Yeah, but I need a cigarette first."

"I thought you quit."

"Yeah, I did, but Joe, my new boyfriend smokes and you know how it is."

"No, I don't Lily May. If you don't want to smoke, then don't."

"Oh, Momma, don't preach to me. I'll quit eventually. I'm goin' out on the back porch."

I watched her through the kitchen window. She dangled the cigarette between red polished finger nails and brushed back her long blonde hair. Such a beautiful girl, I thought. Why does she always pick such loser boyfriends? I wondered about the latest bum.

The long list had started when she was only seventeen. She ran away with the captain of the football team. I remembered the night her father and Sheriff Jim went after them. It was a good thing the law was there, because Tom Senior would have killed the boy. I blamed Lily May more than the young lad. No one could resist her. Sea green eyes and pouty lips had entrapped every boy since first grade. She had the look of an angel and the spirit of a devil. Tom Senior was furious but how could he expect a seventeen year old boy to resist. I never could understand why she chased romance and rainbows with no regard for her future.

After high school graduation, she left for Hollywood. Said she was going to be an actress. She waited tables and married another rainbow chaser. She came home alone four months later needing money for a divorce. We thought she'd learned her lesson and would settle down. But settling down in a small town was not in Lily May's makeup. A few months later she headed back to Hollywood, two more marriages, divorces and several live-ins. Five years ago, she came home for her father's funeral but left immediately after for Las Vegas. More rainbows!

The boys had grown to manhood with much less parenting and more success as adults. They went to college, married, had families and could never come to terms with the behavior of their little sister. And now, all four of them were here to celebrate my birthday and to tell me where to live.

Tom Junior's muscular frame filled the open door way. "Could I get some coffee, Mom?"

"Of course, honey. If the family is awake, I'll start the pancakes."

"No, Mom. We're taking you down town for breakfast. You're not cooking for this crew." He smiled. He was so tall, he could have patted me on the head, but he knew better.

The screen door slammed as Lily May came in reeking of cigarette smoke.

"Still smoking, Sis?"

"You know I am, Birdbrain."

"Now, you two stop it," I said, wiping my hands on my apron front. But the banter had begun.

Lily May looked up at her brother defiantly, "Tell Momma how you used to scare the piss out of me with your stories of ghosts in the cupboard and under the back porch. You were one mean son-of-a-”

“Lily May! None of that talk in this house”.

“Momma, it’s true. He used to tell me the awfulest stories. Whenever the trains went by and shook the house, he said it was ghosts. Ghosts in the cupboards, under the porch and the grass in the back yard, everywhere! You were mean! All three of you guys teased me. You were the brattiest brothers ever.” She ruffled her brother’s hair as he sat at the kitchen table sipping hot coffee.

“I guess it was kind of ornery. But you were so gullible. How could we resist?” He laughed.

“You were a brat! A big mean shit faced brat!”

“Stop!”

“Okay. Okay”. He waved his arms at Lily May to stop her onslaught. “Mom, we need to talk about the Assisted Living condos. Did you have a chance to look over the brochures, we brought you?”

I started to answer but the eight fifteen came barreling through and blasted its horn, so I waited to speak. When the shaking had subsided, calm descended, throughout the house and me. “I probably should wait until the others are up, but you might as well know

now. I'm not going anywhere. I've lived all my life in this small town and most of it in this house by the railroad tracks. I have no need for assistance. I have the neighbor boy to mow, rake and shovel. Old man Trout comes to take care of the storm windows, up in the fall and down in the spring. I certainly have all the social life I can handle, church on Sunday, Bridge every Tuesday and Bingo on Friday. I don't need new friends. The old ones are just fine. I've had most of them since childhood."

"But Momma, the noise. The trains. Your dishes rattle in the cupboard and the back porch is almost falling off from the shaking." Lily May sided with her brother.

Tom Junior was silent. He wasn't used to people disagreeing with him.

I looked around and saw two more sons standing at the kitchen doorway, unsure of what was going on. "You might as well hear too. Come on in and get some coffee."

Pouring the steaming liquid into two mugs, I used my Mom-is-boss- voice, "You boys tormented your little sister with stories about ghosts in the cupboards, on the back porch and everywhere else you could think of. Well, you were right. There are ghosts in this house, all the memories of a happy marriage and children growing up. Your Dad's favorite chair rocks with the vibration on the floor and the beating of my heart. Initials carved in the window sill of a bedroom and the nail holes poked in the walls where teenagers hung pennants are all signs of ghostly presence. The ditch you boys dug for a swimming pool is my flower bed now. And Lily May your bedroom window is still nailed shut. You bet this house is full of ghosts, my ghosts and my memories."

The eight forty five freight came roaring through and I didn't have to explain any more. If they said anything about the benefits of assisted living, I couldn't hear it. When the train finally passed and the tea cups ended their dance in the saucers, I said, "Go home kids. Live your lives and let me finish mine." I turned to face the stove and whispered, "God bless those trains!"

No Tears In Heaven

I relaxed, stretching out in amniotic fluid, listening to my Mothers' heart beat. She pressed her hand against her belly caressing my extended foot. I could hear glasses tinkling in the kitchen sink and water running as she rinsed the dishes. She sang a lullaby in anticipation of my arrival. I felt vibrations as her lungs expanded and pressed against my water world. I loved the sound of her voice. When she laughed, I felt soothing tickles caress my body.

We had been shopping that day. My Grandmother drove. The car made different noises and the motion pushed me from side to side. I didn't have much room. It was almost time for me to be born so my space was crowded. My Mother was tired, but she squealed with giggles when my Grandmother held up a velvet suit for her to admire. "No," my Momma said, "He'll be a T-shirt and jeans boy."

They ate lunch in a noisy restaurant. I could hear my Momma's empty stomach grumble, but soon happy voices lulled me to sleep.

I napped until we got home. I heard the back door slam shut. The man was here again. His voice was loud and angry. I didn't understand the words, but they made my Momma cry. Her sobs shook me. I felt the adrenalin rush through my umbilical cord. I hiccupped and put my thumb in my mouth for comfort. My Momma screamed. The sound reverberated around me. I felt the blow. My Momma lost her balance and I was pushed against her back bone. I heard the crack that broke her neck. The sound of blood coursing through her veins stopped. No heart beat. Silence! I gasped. There was no oxygen in my blood. I kicked. My arms flailed. My heart stopped.

The angels lifted me and gently laid me in my Mother's arms. When I looked into her face, I saw the love of all Mothers, love that lasts through eternity.

I looked down on the kitchen below me. A body lay in a pool of blood, the head twisted to one side like a broken doll. The man kicked her swollen belly and cursed, the words ricocheting off the kitchen tile. His evil soul wore a handsome body, but as I rose in the arms of angels, I could see black mold cover his exterior and the last vestige of goodness leave.

My Mother and I are safe. There are no tears in Heaven.

The Red Barn

He ran his fingers across the bare mahogany desk and looked at the empty book shelves. With a sigh he reviewed an office no longer baring his imprint. Swiveling his chair his gaze fell on the red hibiscus blooming in the courtyard. The deep hued blossom brought back memories of another summer day when he was a boy of twelve, visiting his aunt and uncle on their Montana cattle ranch.

His own home wasn't much different, same sprawling wheat fields, four hundred head of white faced Herefords and too many horses to name. But as an only child, spending the summer with his cousin, Ronald, was a special treat, a time of careless juvenile abandon. Close as brothers, their hours together usually meant adventure or mischief and sometimes both.

The man leaned back in his chair closed his eyes and felt the heat of embarrassment as memory took him back to that bright sunny day of his childhood.

He would never forget the sight of his Uncle Leo, red neckerchief wrapped around his sunburned neck, the sweatband on his Stetson stained with perspiration and an open can of red paint at his feet. "I built this scaffolding around the barn," Leo said. "You can climb up on that ladder at the end. If you start on the west side and paint at a good pace, as you move around, you'll be in the shade all day."

Leo motioned to the boys. "Get on up there and I'll hand you the paint and the brushes."

The man remembered the sinking feeling he felt as a boy when he looked at the size of the barn. It wasn't a boy's plan for fun, but he knew the chore wasn't up for discussion. When Uncle Leo assigned a task, he didn't offer choices. Maybe there would be time for fishing or riding their horses out by the Indian rings later, but for now the old rancher expected work. Leo knew boys were capable of devilment and it would be a job to keep them busy all summer. He'd had experience with these two.

Leo watched them climb into position and handed up the supplies. "See you about noon", he called as he headed for the pickup.

The clapboards on the old barn absorbed the paint thirstily. For half an hour the boys worked. Slap! Slap! Slap! Spatters began to dot the front of their Levis. It was a dull job. Boredom was taking its toll. One quick swipe and the spatters speckled Ronald's face and blonde hair.

"You got freckles," Dave giggled.

Another quick spatter, "So do you, Dave."

"Well, you got red hair."

"So do you." The brushes were flying and both boys were speckled head to toe.

"I'm getting tired of painting up here. Let's go paint the chickens. We'll make Rhode Island Reds out of the White Leghorns."

They scrambled down off the scaffolding, paint bucket in hand. Giggling and running for the chicken yard, they spilled paint leaving a red trail behind them.

The chickens were hard to catch and only a few got dyed to match the barn. There wasn't much paint left in the bucket but the giggling boys were intoxicated by their escapade.

"Let's go paint the pigs. I never saw a red pig, did you?"

They ran to the pig pen. Leaning on the fence, brush in hand, they stretched to paint the muddy snouts. Finding it hard to reach the sow and afraid to climb into her pen, Dave had a better idea.

"Let's go paint the horses. We can make Indian ponies out of them. And have a parade."

They had just finished painting the hooves on poor old "Lady" when they heard the pickup in the driveway. Guilt replaced giggles and fear reminded them that punishment followed mischief.

The man moved gently in his chair as he remembered his uncle's steely blue eyes looking at two paint covered boys and a barn sadly lacking in color. Leo's voice was calm, but the words stuck like a knife in Dave's heart, "I trusted you to do a good job."

That was the moment the boy left childhood behind. No need for any other punishment. He would never forget the words and the lesson. At twelve, he wanted to be a man like Leo and his Dad, men who were respected, men who made cattle deals on a handshake, men who worked the land from dawn to dark and prayed for rain and no hail. Those men would never leave a job half done. It wasn't the red paint or the barn or a mangled chore. His Uncle had trusted him. He had betrayed that trust.

Getting up from his chair, Dave moved over to the window, eyes fastened on the red hibiscus. He whispered, "Uncle Leo, that's the last time I betrayed a trust. I lived my life by the lessons I learned from you and Dad. I've completed every job I started and enjoyed the process of doing it well. After forty years, I'm retiring. My life is changing kind of like it did that day when I was twelve, but I want you to know I still live by those words."

He heard the phone in the outer office and decided it was time to leave. Gathering up his briefcase, he headed out the door. His secretary looked up and said, "Well, how was your last day?" She paused, not really wanting an answer. "Are you looking forward to your retirement dinner tonight?"

"Actually, I was thinking about a red barn."

The Art Lesson

The open doorway framed the dark figure of the old woman, sunlight silhouetting her shape and casting a halo about the wisps of dark hair that had escaped when she pulled the long strands back to form a bun. She stood there hesitantly, not knowing what to do.

My art class was full and had been in session for several weeks. I was a little annoyed. These seniors at the center seemed to think they could come or go as they pleased with no consideration for the time and effort I took to prepare lessons for them.

"Come in. Sign the form at the desk and find a chair." I don't think I even smiled. I continued with my lecture on the techniques for depicting spatial relationships on a flat surface. I felt their drawings would never be realistic if they didn't know the basics of perspective and focal points, but I could tell they were bored by the sound of my voice and just wanted to draw or paint.

Exasperated, I said, "Remember to prioritize the objects in your paintings. Choose the focus of your composition and make the viewer see it as the most important thing in your design. Do it with light, color or line, but don't lead the viewer all over the canvas." I sighed, "Go ahead, paint."

Having found a vacant chair at a table in the back of the room, the old woman took out a small canvas and placed it on her desk top easel. She pulled brushes, paints, a small palette and a jar of water from the tapestry bag she carried. Hunching over her work, she began to paint, not speaking to any of the ladies around her.

Her presence annoyed me. I was still angry from the fight I'd had with Bill that morning at breakfast. We never talked any more. He was too busy with his work and I was too busy with mine. We were drifting apart. We both knew it, but when we did try to talk it always wound up in a fight. I didn't even remember what we were fighting about that morning.

Rubbing my forehead to ease the ache in my head, I surveyed the bowed heads around the room. As soon as their brushes touched the paint, the room became a beehive of artistic activity. I walked up and down the aisles, observing the scenes coming to life on bare white canvases.

When I came to the old woman's desk, I stopped, puzzled by her work. Her canvas was filled with a kaleidoscope of patterns and colors, the figure of an Indian man shown through prisms of light. He was definitely the focal point. There was no scenic distance, but the vibrating colors gave depth to the work. The painting was powerful.

The old woman looked up. Her black eyes seemed to bore holes through me. The wrinkled face and gnarled hands told the story of years of painting on location in the bright sun. I felt warmth flush my cheeks, embarrassed that I really hadn't wanted her in my class. Why was she there? Obviously, she was far more accomplished than the others. She didn't need me for any help with her work.

As I puzzled over her presence she spoke, "Life is like a painting. You get to choose what to make your focal point and what to relegate to the background. It's important that you make the right choice in life. You can't paint over it like you can a canvas."

The old woman picked up her wet canvas and stuffed her paints and brushes in her bag. I was stunned as she walked out the door of the class room, bag over her shoulder and swinging the painting by her side. I looked around at the other students who apparently hadn't noticed her at all.

Curious, I walked over to the sign-in sheet to see what her name was. The line was blank.

Maybe, it was the headache, but I couldn't get the look of those black eyes out of my mind. I didn't realize it then, but that was the beginning of many changes for me.

When I came home that night, I not only heard Bill's voice, but I listened to his heart. He had a job offer that meant leaving the city and moving back to Montana. He bared his soul as he emotionally pled his case. He desperately wanted to take advantage of the opportunity. We needed a change and we both knew it. I embraced the calmness that surrounded me as I agreed.

When blue Montana skies and snow

drifts welcomed us, I prayed we'd made the right choice. I had some doubts, but we'd made the decision together and I was determined to give it a good try.

As spring arrived, I realized our relationship had changed. We had time for each other. Life functioned at a slower pace in Bozeman and Bill loved his job at the university. Our priorities had changed and that old spark had returned.

Months later I was again teaching art, but this time to a group of teenagers. I had become especially friendly with one young Indian girl. Her talent captivated me and I felt her work was destined to someday receive world recognition.

One afternoon, she invited me to her home to meet her family. As her mother graciously led me into the living room, where the aunts and uncles were gathered, I couldn't help but notice a large picture, framed in silver, hanging on the wall. It was a picture of the old woman who had been in my class many months ago.

"Who is that?" I asked my young friend.

"Oh, that's Great Aunt Sophie. She was an artist too. I guess that's where I get my talent. She died before I was born. She lived on the reservation all of her life, but she painted everything she saw. Come I'll show you some of her work."

I barely remember the rest of the afternoon. But I saw with clarity why I'd come to this mountain valley. The lesson the old Indian woman had taught me was burned into my soul. I knew where my focus would always be. There were no doubts. Bill and I would always be together, merged forever into one painting on one canvas.

Little Girl Lost

Maggie shivered in the early morning fog. Still in her bathrobe, she leaned against the railing on the balcony her hands hugging the coffee mug. "I know you're there," she said to the girl. "I don't have to look. I can feel you, dammit." Tears rolled down her cheeks as she turned to face the image. "Why can't you leave me alone? You are a curse, just like Grandma said."

She kicked the crumpled telegram at her feet. "He's gone, you know. The only one I had left. Grandma last spring and now Grandpa. There's nobody, but you. And we both know you're not real. Just my imagination, Grandma always said. A curse! I don't know why Grandpa called you a gift. You always show up at times like this, when I'm at my lowest," she said accusingly.

Maggie remembered the first time she saw the little girl. She wiped her nose with the back of her hand and let the memory fill her thoughts.

It was shortly after her parents were killed in a car accident and she came to live with her grandparents. She remembered the emptiness in her soul; the pain in her gut that wouldn't go away.

Coming home from school that day, she had taken a shortcut through the woods. It wasn't because she wanted to get home sooner. No place felt like home any more.

She had followed a narrow path that led to a clearing surrounded by tall pines and aspens. The afternoon sun, low in the sky, cast a golden light around the figure of a little girl standing in the tall grass. The child appeared to be about eight, the same age as Maggie was then. With eyes too big for her small face and arms hanging limply at her sides she appeared ethereal.

"Who are you?" asked Maggie.

The child didn't answer.

Listening to the waves crashing on the beach below, Maggie sipped her coffee and wondered how many times over the years she had asked the child that question. Silence was always the response.

The first time Maggie saw the child was the only time she ever told anyone of the vision. She had run home that day, slammed the screen door and dropped her books on the floor. Out of breath, she told her grandparents about the girl in the woods.

The memory of her grandparent's angry voices blended with the crashing roar of waves beneath her. Had they been angry before she came or was she the cause? She remembered too many arguments. At thirty five the sound still gave her a chill.

Her Grandmother turned from the kitchen stove and snapped, "There is no little girl. You just imagined her." Remembering the annoyance in her Grandmother's voice, Maggie shivered.

She could almost feel the weight of big hands on her shoulders and Grandpa's face as he looked down at her and said, "It's a gift, Maggie." He smiled and reached to hug her.

"It's not a gift, it's a curse. And don't you go around telling people you saw someone in the woods. They'll think you're daft. You saw nothing!"

Maggie knew there would be no discussion. She never mentioned the child again although she saw her many times.

School was an escape from the tension at home. She had been blessed with teachers who were kind, but Maggie never made close friends. She was a city child, transplanted in farmland, too shy to set down roots.

The school bus brought her to the gravel road that led to her grandparent's farm. She waved goodbye, but no one noticed. Often she listened to her giggling classmates as she left the bus and wished she had a friend. But there was no one except the little girl in the clearing. She always walked home alone.

The phone rang interrupting her thoughts. She knew it would be Gerta, her agent. Oh, God, what will she say?

"Where the hell are you? You were supposed to meet me at the gallery an hour ago."

"I'm not going to the gallery today." Maggie put her hand over the receiver so she couldn't hear the profanity.

"Gerta, my Grandpa died and I'm not going to be at the showing today. I'm going home."

"What the hell? You are home. Send some flowers."

"I need to make arrangements. I'm the only one left."

"Dammit, Maggie. There's a lot of money riding on this show. I've made contacts and I expect to sell plenty of your seascapes. You need to be there. People want to meet the artist when they spend that kind of money. Call a lawyer and let him handle the arrangements. I know Montana is a wilderness, but my God, they must have attorneys there."

"You can sell my stuff without me, Gerta. You could sell a tuxedo to a monkey. Don't give me that kind of crap. I'm going home. I'll call you when I get there."

Maggie was shaking when she hung up the phone. She had never spoken to anyone with that kind of authority, and certainly never to Gerta. She turned to look at the balcony and the little girl was gone.

She caught a flight out of LAX and rented a car in Missoula. The drive down the Bitterroot Valley brought back painful memories but as each one surfaced and the miles passed, she realized that she was a woman, not the little girl who tried to please everyone and who shared an existence with an imaginary child in the woods.

By the time she reached Darby and the

turnoff to the farm, the tears had dried on her cheeks and she could hardly wait to see the old farm house. When she came to the woods, she stopped the car. The wheels dug into the gravel. She waited for the dust to settle. She had to see the little girl. The path was the same. Did animals keep it open? The child was there, sunlight shining through her golden hair. A sense of serenity surrounded the girl.

"I know who you are. You're me, my soul. I'm not afraid any more. Come into my heart where you belong."

That was the last time Maggie saw the little girl. She never went back to Los Angeles. Gerta was furious until Maggie sent her painting of snow capped mountains and lush valleys, wild buffalo and tranquil deer. There was a peacefulness that hadn't existed in her work before. The paintings sold for a lot of money, so Gerta was happy.

Maggie finally understood what her Grandparents meant. The little girl had been a curse and a gift. When life was too difficult to bear, Maggie set her soul apart so her own heart wouldn't break. Now she was at peace, now she was whole.

Lift Your Feet To Fly

The sound of the explosion pierced my ears and reverberated in my gut. A wooden beam slammed against my shoulders and knocked me to my knees. Plaster and brick came crashing down and buried me in darkness. Screams mingled with the incessant bursts of gunfire. Sergeant Conner's voice barked orders over the din. Pain stole my breath. I gulped. Tears burned my eyes and streaked my face. I couldn't cry. I was a man. I was eighteen.

I drifted into a silent world. Was it hallucinations? I didn't care. My grandpa's voice beckoned. "We need to milk the cows. Grandma has breakfast waiting."

I smelled bacon and biscuits.

He scolded. “You’ve got to stop being such a dreamer, Barney. Get your head out of that book and help me tend to the chores.”

Sun beams danced across the checkered tablecloth. Bananas and oranges filled the chipped fruit bowl and three places were set. I could see the farm kitchen and my grandma’s back as she stood at the stove turning eggs in a cast iron frying pan.

“Why does Grandpa always scold me for reading?”

“Work has to get done, Barney. You can read after you tend to the cows. Grandpa can’t do it all.”

“But Grandma.”

She was gone. I was in the barn. The smell of cows and hay mixed with manure filled my nostrils. The cats meowed. Grandpa squirted milk in their direction. My old Tom cat stood on his feet and danced as the warm liquid hit his face and whiskers. I wanted to laugh, but I couldn’t.

I felt a burning searing pain in my back! Screams! Were they mine? I wasn’t in the barn any more. The ground shook. More explosions! Sergeant Conners’ voice roared, “God dammit, Barney. Lift your feet. I ain’t leavin’ you here.”

I slipped away again. I'm cold. My book is open and Grandma's afghan is wrapped around me, but the freezing air is coming in around the windows. It must be winter. Please, Grandpa, no chores. Someday I'll be an astronaut or a pilot. I'm not just a dreamer. Someday, I will fly.

"Barney, have you done your homework?"

"In a minute. Grandma."

"Now! Barney, put that book away and get to your homework." Her voice was cross.

"I'm cold, Grandma. I'm so cold."

"Barney, you've got to stop being such a dreamer. There's work to do." She scolded but the love in her voice cooed soft and sweet.

"Move your butt. Lift your feet. Dammit, soldier! I ain't leaving you here." The gravelly voice demanded obedience and broke into my reverie but the chill stayed with me. I shivered.

Men cursed and yelled the names of their buddies and cried out for their mommas. Their voices meshed with the sounds of trucks and tanks. I felt strong arms and hands pull at my shoulders, but the beams held me tight. Pain pushed me towards the vision of the farm and the voices of my grandparents, but Sergeant Conner's voice boomed an oath. "Lift your feet, dammit, lift your feet."

I remembered Grandpa's voice as he admonished me not to be a dreamer all my life. "Boy, if you want to succeed, you gotta get your nose out of that book and your butt off that couch. Son, you gotta lift your feet to fly."

I understood. The pain shot up my leg and back. I moved my foot and felt strong hands pull me up and out.

The doctors amputated my mangled foot. I didn't have to dream of the farm and my grandparents any more. The Army sent me home.

As a boy, I had a vision. Someday I would be an astronaut or a pilot. As a man, I understood the lesson my grandparents taught me. It takes work to achieve any goal. You gotta lift your feet to fly. And I will.

Lessons Learned

"You cannot write things like this," she said. "How dare you write that Sister Amata flirts with the teenage boys in her class? How dare you voice such trash? What will people think of you? Of me?"

I didn't hear the rest. Her voice droned on, but I the only thing I heard was, "You cannot write." And I believed her.

Kneeling on the hearth, I watched her tear the sheets from my notebooks and fling them one by one into fireplace. The flames licked the edges of the paper and turned them golden brown as they curled and fell through the grates, a soft gray mass. Ashes! My Mother's voice was measured, not loud. She never yelled. She didn't have to. She had the same authority as God.

I cried for my loss, my first attempt at writing a novel. "You cannot write!" The words cut through my soul and shaved parts of it away.

I knew my Mother's position in our small Montana community depended on perfect behavior, perfect children. The morals clause in her teaching contract demanded that there be no blemish on her reputation. It was 1945, my Father was dead. She needed that job and I had crossed a forbidden line, writing about flirtatious nuns, priests who drank too much and a teenager's sexual romp in the back seat of a Chevy. Exaggerated tales gleaned from girl's locker room talk and teenage observations. We didn't even talk about such things, much less write about them. "How could I besmirch the good name of my teachers and friends," she asked.

I wondered if she recognized them. But I knew better than speak. Was it so poorly written that she was ashamed? It must have been, because I heard the words, "You cannot write!"

It had been a lonely summer. We were in Minneapolis, staying with my Great Aunt who was dying of cancer. I hated the smell of antiseptic that permeated the big old two story house. Doctors and nurses bustled in and out, ignoring everyone but their patient. I missed my dog and my friends in Montana. I was bored.

I'd lost interest in writing my journal, so one Sunday after Mass, I headed for the attic. I wasn't sure just what I was looking for, but anything would be better than polite greetings to Auntie's doctor.

I was sick of old people. But I liked the old house. I was sure it had stories to tell. The walnut paneled entry hall and carved newel posts on the front stairs beckoned to me. The aroma of furniture oils filled the foyer as I headed for the second floor and took the back stairs to the attic.

Trunks lined the outer walls. Sunlight shown through the windows at the far end revealing books stacked neatly beneath on the hard wood floor. A single bulb hung from a cord in the center of the gabled space. I grabbed a pillow from an open box and made myself comfortable near the light. At first, I just wanted to read, but ideas kept bouncing around my head. I decided to write my own story.

Every day I disappeared to the attic taking a notebook with me. No one seemed to notice. My Great Aunt was too sick and my Mom was too busy. By the end of summer I had filled three notebooks with my story. My characters were thinly disguised friends and teachers from my school. Who else could I write about? At sixteen, they were the only people I knew.

I learned an important lesson that day as I watched the flames turn my papers to ashes. The spoken word has tremendous power. It can dissect the heart in an instant and as quickly comfort a broken one. But, it was much later that I realized that teenagers only hear part of what is said to them. They have a filter that stops the sound and misconstrues the meaning when an adult speaks. The only part of my Mother's admonition I heard was those devastating three words, "You cannot write."

The day after the burning, I packed my suitcase to return to Montana and school. Shirts and socks went into the big bag, but I placed the words in a small one to carry with me. They were part of my permanent baggage.

I was an old lady before the clasp on that bag broke sending torrents of words spilling out. Three words had held me captive for many years. At sixteen I could not speak, but finally, I found my voice. My response is, "I cannot stop."

Betty Grayce

Purple Ink And Five Bathrooms

The dog barked when the mailman came up the front walk. I heard the mail hit the tile floor by the door slot. My hands were in soapy dishwater so I grabbed a towel and ran to catch my two year old. He would gladly eat or tear up anything on the floor. The race was a tie, but I managed to grab the letters with both hands. Bobby screamed and reached for the treasure he felt he'd earned.

"Want a cookie?"

His hands were waving in the air but the yelling stopped when he heard the magic word, "cookie".

He followed me to the kitchen and sat on the floor to munch his favorite snack. When I dumped the pile of mail on the table, the letter with purple ink peeked out behind the electric bill. I shivered. No one I ever knew but Marcella Burton used purple ink. Suddenly, I felt fifteen again. It had been ten years since jealousy had ruled my life. I looked at the address scrawled in the handwriting I knew had to be hers. Little circles ended her sentences and heart shapes decorated the margins. No one else wrote like that. It had to be Marcella.

The memory of that cold November weekend made me shiver. I had been envious of her from the first day of class in the fall. Her family had moved into the old Anderson house, the big one on the hill at the end of Maple Street. It had seven bedrooms and five bathrooms. My friends and I giggled that there were more potties than people in that house. With five kids, my family could have used a second one, but on my Dad's teacher's salary the budget included things like food and shoes. I was used to hearing, "We can't afford it." It didn't bother me too much until Marcella moved to town. I wished I lived in a big house like hers and had a charge card for Kitty's Boutique down town.

Marcella was different from the rest of us. She not only lived in the fanciest house in town, at fifteen she had a self awareness that we lacked. It wasn't just because she was pretty. There was a mystery about her. Those blue eyes could look into your soul. She wanted to know everything about us. She listened as we babbled about our lives. Within a month, she knew everyone in school.

The boys hung around her hoping to be noticed. We were jealous of the male attention so it was social self defense when we girls took over, including her in our clique. It was hard not to like her. She was nice, but envy was a barrier to true friendship.

The Friday she invited me to her house for a sleepover, I couldn't wait to tell my friends.

"Why'd she invite you," they asked in unison.

"I don't know. But I'll tell you all about it. What do you think her room will be like?" I could see their sullen faces. "Look, she just wants to get better acquainted. It's no big deal. Her folks probably wouldn't let all of us come at once. She'll probably ask you guys next time." I rushed off to class to get away from the betrayal in their eyes.

I wanted to see the inside of the big house. I tried to ease my conscience by telling myself that Marcella was a friend and that was the only reason I was going to the sleepover. But I knew better. I salivated thinking about the ornamentations that would be in that house, maybe, woven carpets from Egypt or carved ivory from China, furniture and art I'd only read about. I was going to see how rich people lived. Five bathrooms! It had nothing to do with Marcella. I wanted to be a rich girl. I was willing to pretend friendship to get what I wanted. I was thankful to be the one she asked.

The school bus let us off at the corner. We waved goodbye to the other girls and headed up the long walk to the front of the house. It was almost Thanksgiving and the trees were bare with patches of snow covering parts of the lawn and driveway. The white pillars were taller than they had appeared from the street. The carved mahogany door reached at least nine feet. The side windows were long and narrow, the crystal prisms of glass reflecting the afternoon sun. I was disappointed when she said, "Come around to the back. I never go in the front door."

"Okay," I said and looked over my shoulder at the beautiful facade. The portal beckoned but I followed my host's instructions. As we walked along the side of the house, I noticed that all the windows were draped, completely closed to any daylight. Strange, I thought. My Mom always opened the blinds first thing in the morning. Of course we weren't rich like Marcella's family.

When we entered the kitchen, the room was dark. I felt a chill. Nothing cooking, I thought. Not like my house where the aroma of fresh baked cookies greeted me when I opened the back door. My Mom's apron was usually smeared with cinnamon and brown sugar as we sat around the kitchen table jabbering about our day. With five kids it was noisy.

Marcella said, "Don't touch anything. We'll go upstairs to my room and have some snacks."

"Where's your Mom?" It was an innocent question.

"She's resting. We'll see her at dinner."

We didn't go into the living room so I don't know if there were any paintings or woven rugs there, but as we passed the study I saw gold bound volumes on shelves behind a big desk. But the room was too dark to make out any carving on the wood front. I felt like I was being dragged through a museum and not allowed to look.

The somber darkness disappeared when Marcella opened the door to her room. White furniture and pink walls defined her space. Flowered chintz pillows adorned the four poster bed. A TV cabinet with bookshelves on either side lined one wall. And she didn't have to share it with two sisters. I thought only a princess would have a bedroom like this.

Remembering the jealousy I felt that afternoon, I shivered and went to get Bobby another cookie. I had to open the letter but I couldn't forget that night.

I did see Marcella's mother at dinner. But someone else cooked the meal and served it. Marcella's Mom sat at the head of the table. Her peach silk dress was cut low to reveal the curves of her bosom. Dark brown hair fell in soft waves allowing her diamond earrings to catch the light as she moved her head. I thought she looked like the movie stars we saw at the Saturday matinee. The ice in her glass tinkled as she leaned forward and in a husky voice said, "And what was your name, dear?" She asked me three times so I thought maybe she was hard of hearing.

Marcella's Dad didn't come home. I guessed rich people didn't eat together like my family always did. At my house we held hands around the dining room table while my Dad said grace. Sometimes one of us kids got to say the prayer, usually if we had done something special like getting an "A" in algebra or making a home run. One winter my brother got to say grace every day for a week because he shoveled the snow off Widow Johnson's front sidewalk without being asked and he wouldn't take any money for it. He got lots of praise for that. We laughed a lot too. You don't have to be rich to laugh. I guessed my family was different because we were poor.

After supper Marcella and I went back to her room. We watched TV and talked about the boys at school. I heard voices and figured Marcella's father had come home. It was close to midnight when we finally gave up and went to sleep.

The screams woke me. I sat up in bed. Another scream! Something crashed against the wall. "What was that? Marcella, wake up."

She groaned and pulled the pillow over her head.

A man's voice yelled, "You little bitch! I could kill you."

More screams and yells.

I got out of bed and opened the door a little

crack.

"I could kill you and no one would ever know!"

Terrified, I crept over to the bed and shook Marcella's shoulder.

"Someone is going to kill somebody. We've gotta do something."

She sat up in bed. "It's just my parents. They get mad and they say things. Go back to bed. It's nothing." She pulled the pillow over her head.

I crawled back into my side of the bed and listened to the harangue. Two people screaming and furniture crashing, how could Marcella sleep?

"I've got a gun. I'm not taking this from you any more."

It sounded like a firecracker, but I knew it wasn't. There were more screams as I sneaked down the hall to the phone in the kitchen. I called the police and shivered in my nightgown as I waited by the front door.

Mr. Watkins, my neighbor and family friend was one of the policemen who came. He got a blanket from the squad car and wrapped it around my shoulders. He hugged me and told me to wait in the back seat of the car. I wanted to go home. I wasn't jealous of

Marcella any more. I liked my house better.

I tore the envelop open and there was that familiar handwriting. We hadn't seen much of each other after that fateful Friday. Her Mom went to the hospital and eventually recovered from the beating and her Dad went to anger management classes. They both went to AA but the talk around town was they still liked their Johnny Walker. They moved away that spring. I heard he ran for Judge on a Family Value Platform up in North County but he lost.

After they moved Marcella wrote, but gradually the letters became infrequent. We both went to the state university and I saw her from time to time. I'm not sure she ever forgave me for calling the police that night. We never talked about it. I realized there were more differences about us that just rich or poor.

I opened the letter and read aloud. I don't know why. My two year old wasn't interested.

Dear Joanie,

We never talked about the night you called the police. I was too ashamed. I don't know why, but kids of alcoholics feel somehow their parents' drinking is their fault.

I wanted parents like yours. I wanted a house with love and laughter. I was so jealous of you. I knew the girls joked about all the bathrooms in my house but five bathrooms don't make a home. It takes a Mom and Dad who are sober enough to care.

I figured I must be bad and I deserved to live with all that anger. I know now that my parents' drinking was their doing and not mine.

You saved their lives that night. My Mom would have killed my Dad. And she would have gone to prison. I want you to know it was the last beating she took. She got her life back when she left my Dad and gave up the bottle. Dad passed away last spring of cirrhosis.

I wanted to let you know that I'm free of guilt. I was not to blame for their problem, but I never had the courage to tell anyone and get them help. I thank you for doing that for me.

I got married last summer and we are expecting our first child. I should say children. We're having twins. I thought you'd like to know that our house is like yours was. One bathroom and lots of love.

Marcella

I put the letter on the table and kissed my two year old's crumb covered face. Lifting Bobby high in the air I said, "Momma's gonna bake a chocolate cake. You don't know it sweetie, but your Momma's rich and that has nothing to do with bathrooms." I'd known for a long time that I was the one who was wealthy and always had been. I think the only word he understood was "chocolate", but that was enough. He squealed with glee.

Betty Grayce

Silent Feathered Wings

Before I reached the top of the steps and looked down at the silver slide, I knew I was in trouble. I wanted to turn around and climb back down but there were too many kids behind me yelling, "Go, go, go." Terrified I slipped my feet over the top and slid into the wide channel that delivered me to the churning waters of Riverside Lake. Plunging into the cold water, I sank like a rock to the bottom. I squirmed as the sedge wrapped its sinuous arms around my legs and pulled me deep into the sediment. The more I struggled, the tighter its grip. Looking through the water above me, I could see the light, but there was no air to breathe. Then blackness engulfed me. The angel didn't come. Neither did the devil.

The man's hands hurt my back as he forced the lake water from my lungs. The vomit stung my throat and the sand felt rough against my cheek. I felt the angel's cool hand brush the hair from my face and I relaxed. I knew she was there.

Someone yelled, "Get that dog out of here." But Mickey stood his ground. He barked his response.

My brother and his friends swam from the raft floating off shore. They came to see what was going on. What was all the excitement? The boys knew they'd be in trouble. They were supposed to be watching me, the seven year old who couldn't swim.

I don't remember the ride to the hospital, but I know I said, "Not without my dog." They didn't listen. Grownups never do.

Childhood, that short powerless time, shapes our souls. As a lathe carves a block of wood with deep groves and rounded curves, so our fears and pleasures are cut deep into the psyche. The warm summer day at the lake, and the blackness at its depths etched a fear that dwells deep within me. I won't forget that a barking dog and an unseen angel were responsible for my rescue.

I first met my angel at an old brick school

where the nuns in black habits and black beads swinging from their waists ruled with unforgiving power. I sat in a chair too big swinging my feet and listening to tales of God and Satan. The teacher's voice rose and fell with a roaring crescendo followed by a soft menacing whisper. My heart remembers the beat as it matched the rhythm of her throaty proclamations. I had to look away to avoid a hypnotic trance. The image of fire and the vortex it created pulled me toward its depth.

But I would not be captured. My eyes scanned the room looking for my guardian angel. The picture of her, golden hair and white feather wings, hung on the wall. I felt her presence and took her hand. Attentively, I sat in my chair, the obedient child, but I let my angel lead me to a garden of my imagination where flowers bloomed and color abounded. We traveled down a gravel path, the stones crunching beneath my feet, and the sound of chirping birds in my ears. She held my hand and cradled in the comfort of her touch, I felt safe.

My angel went everywhere with me. She loved the ivy covered stone of the Carnegie library building. Inside the book filled shelves stretched from floor to ceiling. The smell of drying pages and faded ink made me sneeze but that was where the gates to my imagination opened. Climb the ladder! Get books from the top shelf! Sit on a wooden chair! Read! Stay until the librarian shows you the door. The angel understood and she egged me on.

How many dogs does it take to fill a lifetime? I learned the joy of my existence each time a fat bellied puppy with green grass breath licked my face and the pain of loss when one died. The border collies grew old listening to my childish conversations and gave me comfort with tail wags. They spoke to me as my angel did.

No longer a child, I became the girl who rode horses across the prairie with her best friend, the boy who stole my heart and kept it for over fifty years. I remember the sensation of long hair blowing across my face as we rode up and down coulees looking for sleeping deer. The aroma of sage and pine mingled with the smell of cattle grazing in open pastures. We ate picnic lunches under cottonwood trees and told our deepest secrets as we bared our souls to each other. We fell in love.

We married, had children. With nails and bricks we built a house. With love and compassion we build a home. Like a tartan of worsted wool dyed with vibrant color, we wove the threads of family unity and strength together.

You cannot hear her fly, but with silent feathered wings, I know she is there. The guardian angel, whose hand held mine, still watches over me.

Order Blank
(for additional copies of this book)
Add $17.45 for each copy

Fill out this page and mail with your charge card no. or check made payable to:
To: David Kalfell
GoForBooks
27069 Bottlebrush Lane
Sun City, CA 92586-208

Number of Copies ____________________

Name: ____________________________

Address __________________________

City, St. Zip _______________________

Phone ____________________________

Charge card Type ___________________

Number ___________________________

Expiration _________________________

Printed in the United States
37770LVS00002B/213

9 781890 461263